THE
LAVENDER
DRAGON

THE
LAVENDER
DRAGON

Eden Phillpotts

Dover Publications, Inc.
Mineola, New York

Bibliographical Note

This Dover edition, first published in 2017, is an unabridged republication of the work originally published by The Macmillan Company, New York, in 1923.

International Standard Book Number

ISBN-13: 978-0-486-81725-5
ISBN-10: 0-486-81725-3

Manufactured in the United States by LSC Communications
81725301   2017
www.doverpublications.com

THE
LAVENDER
DRAGON

Starla L Stocking

Contents

I	PONGLEY-IN-THE-MARSH	1
II	THE APPOINTMENT FOR RAINBARROW	10
III	VIGIL	19
IV	THE DRAGON KEEPS HIS WORD	22
V	THE DRAGON EXPLAINS	26
VI	THE DRAGON GOES ON EXPLAINING	38
VII	GREAT NEWS FOR GEORGE PIPKIN	49
VIII	THREE SONGS AND A STORY	58
IX	ANOTHER DRAGON GIVES A LOUDER ROAR	73
X	FROM JOY TO WOE	79
XI	THE PASSING	86
XII	BUTTERFLIES	94

I

PONGLEY-IN-THE-MARSH

NIGH ABOUT the middle of the Dark Ages, when ignorance, greed
and superstition largely ruled the world, pretty much in fact as do
these forces at present, a knight and his squire proceeded to their
destination under the setting sun. Sir Jasper de Pomeroy, descendant
of that distinguished man who assisted William the Conqueror, and
received for his service fair hundreds in the County of Devon, was
a youth who favoured his English mother and betrayed little of the
Norman in his appearance or composition. He conformed to a style
formerly regarded as noble and now considered somewhat fatuous.
His architecture befitted the times and was Gothic, supple and exquisite. The knight's hair flashed golden in the evening sunshine; his
eyes were large, prominent and very blue; his complexion, though
warmed to ruddiness by outdoor life, had naturally been pink and
white. He wore a heavy amber moustache, which often caught in the
mouthpiece of his helmet and gave him a painful tweak. His nose
had a lofty bridge and his brow was high but wanted breadth. The
purest ideals, combined with a profound lack of humour, character-
ised Sir Jasper's quality. He resembled an admirable mother; and his
father, a man of average ability and more than average selfishness,
had bluntly told the young fellow that he possessed a heart of gold
and a brain of clay. Weighing the criticism without resentment, Sir
Jasper, determined on his career, took all the proper vows, and ded-
icated himself to the service of knight errantry.

He now approached the conclusion of his first circuit, and, up to the present, nothing of any note had challenged his knightly courage, or offered an obstacle to his uneventful progress. His squire, George Pipkin, was a plain dealer of large experience. He had filled similar appointments on former occasions, seen life and felt it, for he chanced to be unhappily married. A grizzled, lean Yorkshireman of fifty was George, and since Sir Jasper enjoyed great wealth and entertained the highest opinion of his supporter, the squire felt well satisfied of his present employ. The better was he pleased, because their expedition, now drawing to its close, had encountered no hardships and proceeded with reasonable comfort, smiled upon by good weather, devoid of any adventure whatsoever.

Sir Jasper rode a magnificent stallion with large chestnut markings on a white ground. In the Middle Ages a circus was not known, and therefore your piebald horse awakened no anticipation of merriment. Nor, in any case, had the knight been a man to find amusement in the color of his steed. As for George Pipkin, he bestrode an elderly roan, as tough and wiry and experienced as himself.

The elder was talking as they traversed rough tracks of moorland, which ceased suddenly at an edge of limestone crags. Beneath these boundaries there subtended fertile plains, ran a river, and stood an attractive hamlet with gabled roof-trees and white-washed walls.

"What makes life picturesque," declared the squire, "are the people who prefer their own experience to that of others—such men as yourself, Sir Jasper. But those who trust tradition and the accumulated wisdom of the race, go farther, are generally more satisfactory and invariably more prosperous members of society. They are safe and therefore rather dull to watch; while the adventurer, who casts loose for good or ill, is nearly always entertaining. Not that his experiences will be novel, or probably outside our own; but the freshness and charm of the spectacle he presents lie in the fact that familiar, old things are happening to a new spirit, unarmed against them with the trite weapons of precaution. Such a young man's retort to the primitive tests of love, danger, temptation and so forth cannot be foretold. Hence every one of his adventures has the charm of novelty."

"Do not imagine, George, that I flout tradition," answered the younger. "My grandfather was a famous knight without fear or reproach. Indeed, my father devotes such leisure as he allows himself from the business of money-making and enjoyment of luxury, to writing a full and punctual account of Sir Hugo de Pomeroy's attractive career."

"Yes, he does; and that is the difference between you and your parent," answered Pipkin. "He sees no charm in a suit of steel and the life that you have adopted. He feels it far more convenient to write of another's devotion to high causes than seek high causes himself; while you, on the contrary, would emulate your famous ancestor."

Sir Jasper sighed.

"Would that I might," he replied. "The world has changed since his romantic day. The times are tame, George. The giants are dead and the dragons have fled; not a robber baron to chastise; not a village to rescue out of tyranny; not a maiden in need of succour from her oppressors."

"We never know our greatest blessings," replied Pipkin. "Many a knight has rued the day when he rescued a fair damsel. I need not repeat the story of a former master, Hildebrand of the Iron Forehead. You recollect particulars of his married life. When he passed to glory, under the scimitars of a thousand Saracens, there was a smile of pure happiness on his forbidding features. As for my own career, had I not wedded his lady's serving maid, I should be a home-staying man at this moment."

"Be sure that your wife will welcome you with awakened affection when you see her again, next September," said Sir Jasper kindly; but George Pipkin shook his head.

"For the most part," he answered, "marriage is like following the ocean. What married man, or mariner, would not change his state if he could do so? But they plunge into wedlock, or go down to the sea in ships, as the case may be, and only regret it once, and that is for ever afterwards."

They had now reached the declivities, and Sir Jasper smiled at the scene of rural peace and beauty extended in the valley beneath them.

George drew a roll of paper from his wallet and consulted a rough map, made by the innkeeper with whom they had lodged on the previous night.

"This will be Pongley-in-the-Marsh," he said. "A populous hamlet apparently and good, no doubt, for comfortable quarters."

"A place without a care as far as one may judge," declared Sir Jasper, surveying the smiling thorpe. "Still we will proceed, as ever, with enthusiasm to inspire and hope to guide."

The sun flamed upon his splendid figure and flashed along his armour and crested helm, so that it seemed a shooting-star descended the bridle-path into the valley. Indeed, an object so conspicuous could not be missed even by peasant eyes, and when, half an hour later, the knight and his companion approached the outskirts of Pongley-in-the-Marsh, he perceived some concourse of the folk.

George Pipkin frowned, for his experienced eyes feared a deputation, and a deputation usually meant labour at no distant date.

Some fifty people, of rustic and humble pattern, approached Sir Jasper, and at the head of the company marched a majestic, old man who bore a staff of office. He wore homespun garments, but was decorated with a chain round his neck and a badge upon his breast. His long, white hair curled about his stooping shoulders, and he appeared a little nervous, for his mouth worked tremulously.

"Welcome to Pongley-in-the-Marsh, most noble knight," he said. "We are your servants, Sire, one and all, and beg that you will accept such simple but ample hospitality as we can offer, and such comfort as we know. The best we have is yours to command."

Sir Jasper felt gratified, for the country folk were not wont to receive him thus, and George Pipkin stepped forward to rehearse in a loud voice his master's style and title.

"Sir Jasper de Pomeroy," he concluded, "rides the world to right all wrong, redress all grievance and place his sword and his lance at the service of the humblest sufferer, be he noble or simple. Therefore, if there are any among you who smart undeservedly, or endure evil within the power of a doughty knight to defeat, let him speak, that

Sir Jasper of the Silver Lance may judge whether his cause be such as to claim right, as well as might, and unchain his unconquerable puissance upon the side of God and man."

The ancient Portreeve of Pongley bowed to the earth, and the company behind him did the like. A rabblement of urchins were driven back, and a mongrel dog, who dared to sniff at the heels of Sir Jasper's piebald steed, received a kick and howled unmelodiously. When silence had been restored, the old man spoke.

"Never have we heard a more gracious message, or welcomed a rarer knight," he declared. "My name, Sir Jasper de Pomeroy, is Jacob Pratt, and I am master here by accordant vote of my friends and neighbours. You come to us at a moment when trouble and concern are heavy in the land, and when, despite the promise of good harvest and other propitious signs, we are cast into deep tribulation. For years we have suffered from a melancholy scourge, and but a week ago, after periods of peace, the evil broke forth again and our inveterate enemy has struck in the tenderest quarter and robbed us of the fairest maiden who ever brightened Pongley-in-the-Marsh with her radiant presence. In a word, Sir Knight, there is a dragon of formidable proportions and utmost malevolence, who abides in an impenetrable lair but a league and a half from this unhappy hamlet. From time to time he breaks upon us in our most secure hours and snatches from our midst now one citizen and now another. Not only men, but women and orphan children he devours; and such is his incredible cunning, that though our trained bands have often marched against him, he evades their sallies and is never faced save by unarmed and helpless persons. He flies through the air on immense pinions, but at a height invariably beyond bow-shot; nor would any cloth-yard shaft pierce the monster—of that be sure. Only once within my memory has an errant knight ever before visited Pongley; but nothing came of it; and we pray on our bended knees that you may have a stouter courage and better appetite to rid us of this cruel tyrant than had he."

Sir Jasper's eyes sparkled as he turned to Pipkin.

"My vade-mecum, George," he said, and on receiving a little, well-thumbed volume, he turned to the index and looked up "Dragons."

"These misbegotten monsters are few," he told them. "I find here not above six or seven right, authentic dragons left in the land of the living, and of these four flourish abroad—two in Italy, one in France, and one in the Holy Land. We still appear to have 'a great Worm' in the Peak and—yes, 'The Lavender Dragon' of Yorkshire!"

"The Lavender Dragon! The Lavender Dragon!" cried the inhabitants of Pongley in melancholy chorus.

"He is our accursed foe, Sir Jasper," explained Jacob Pratt. "He dwells some ten miles distant, amidst the impenetrable Woods of Blore, and from Caytor Fell good eyes may see a huge wall that circles his domain and strange, barbaric buildings of enormous size erected therein. For the monster is no cave-dweller, or laidly wretch, who lives beneath the earth. To such a measure of understanding has he attained, that he dares to assume human manners, lives in a castle and hides his iniquities behind cyclopean masonry. In fact, he is a dragon with a brain—the most perilous combination of mind and matter it is possible to imagine. For his intelligence only lends power to his ferocity, and though he may dwell in a castle and ape his betters, he does not scruple to destroy the sons and daughters of mankind and behave otherwise after the horrible custom of his own species."

"My perambulation draws to a close," replied Sir Jasper, "and it is a source of the keenest satisfaction to me that Providence has seen fit to guide my charger's steps to this secluded spot. We will sup with you, Jacob Pratt, and accept the best that your means afford; and at the dawn of another day, having heard particulars, we will set forth into the marches of the Lavender Dragon and draw not rein until either he, or ourselves, have returned to the merciful Father of us all."

Upon which welcome assurance, Sir Jasper and his squire proceeded among a joyful gathering into the village. After supper and before he retired for the night, the fearless lad sat by a fire of peat and listened to his host's discourse, while George, in an adjoining chamber, overhauled the hero's armour, his sword and his famous Silver Lance, all grown a little rusty from long disuse.

The Portreeve perceived that he had to do with a brave and stalwart hero; but he threw no shadow on the immense difficulties of the enterprise.

"A high soul and a trusty spear are only the first essentials," he ventured to say. "Craft must be met with craft, your honour, and cunning with cunning. He is a dragon of great age and vast experience. It is vain to suppose that no knight until now has tackled the ruffian; and as he still flourishes like the green bay tree, we are to fear that he has triumphed on previous occasions, when justice demanded another issue to the conflict. Too well we know, in this hard world, that might is often allowed to conquer right—doubtless for heavenly purposes by us not understood."

Sir Jasper nodded.

"It is idle to blink facts," he confessed. "One hears of our knightly triumphs, but the troubadours seldom sing those unhappy failures which tact conceals, though knowledge cannot deny. The dragon you say lies hidden upon the path of solitary individuals and spirits them away?"

"We have reason to believe that he devours them in situ," answered Jacob Pratt. "So far as we can judge, the monster consumes them as we eat a radish, for not a fragment of mortality, not a garment, not a cap, not a tag, or shoestring, ever remains to tell the tale. Dusk is his happy hunting hour, and such as wander in the gloaming of dawn or night take their lives into their hands. Sometimes a scream is heard and the hurtle of his infernal wings and the scent of lavender, which always accompanies his progress by land and air. Then that lonely soul is gone for ever. He has a strange art to choose the widow, or the widower, and such as lack for friends or substance. As I have told you, an orphan possesses a horrible fascination for him, and children he cannot resist even in the noon of day. For many years he was but an evil legend; but of late his activities increase. Within my experience, as Portreeve of Pongley, he has snapped Thomas Fagg, the woodman; Nicol Prance, the thatcher; old John Cobbley, a swineherd; and Hugh Hobanob, the baker's man. Of females we have lost Avisa Snell and her child—devoured together; Mary Fern, a good girl, who lost her man in the wars; Betsy Snow, a widow; Jenifer Mardle, another widow; and, only last week, Lilian Lovenot, the belle of the village and the noblest, worthiest, loveliest maiden that ever gladdened the eyes of her fellow creatures. Her parents are both dead, or I should say her foster parents, for there is a mystery attaching to her birth, and we have never believed that such a homely pair as Peter and Nancy Lovenot could have begotten so distinguished a child as Lilian. But now she, too, has been snatched away, and as for the children, both boys and girls that he has laid his claws upon, their numbers can hardly be remembered. Thus our cup of grief is full, and you will guess with what gratitude we learn that you will destroy this abomination, or perish in the attempt."

Sir Jasper pulled his great moustache, drank another stoup of metheglin and looked thoughtfully at the fire.

"What manner of knight was he of whom you spoke when first we met?" he inquired.

"One Sir Rollo Malherbe," replied the Portreeve; "but——"

"Enough," said George Pipkin, who had joined them for a drink; "if that gallant gentlemen indeed learned that a formidable dragon was wasting your quarters, it is certain that he put no great tax upon the hospitality of Pong-ley-in-the-Marsh."

"He stayed but four and twenty hours," admitted Jacob Pratt. "On the morrow of his arrival he set forth, conducted by our valiant young men, and beheld the Lavender Dragon roaming at will along the Valley of Red Rocks, a favourite haunt nigh the Woods of Blore. One glance, at a distance of half a mile, proved enough for Sir Rollo. He remembered him of a fire-drake which he had undertaken to slay somewhere in the South Riding, many leagues distant, and, saying that he must keep faith, but would return at an early date, spurred his charger and was never seen again."

"Your fire-drake, or hippogriff, is found but six to ten feet long," mused Sir Jasper, "whereas your right dragon may number six hundred feet—or more."

"Our enemy is computed to be perhaps five and thirty rods from beak to tail," said the Portreeve's right-hand man—a little, plump fellow with a cane-coloured beard and fat, pock-marked cheeks. "He is of a coerulean blue colour, having a rich rosy sheen in direct sunlight; and when he spreads his pinions they are as a flower-garden for beauty, being all shades of emerald and azure, purple and gold. In truth a lovelier beast God never made; yet within this fair and glittering carcase there hides the heart of a crocodile and the brain of a demon."

"It would seem that I have my work cut out for me," said Sir Jasper grimly.

"Fear nothing, noble knight. All Pongley will be upon its knees at the first moment of onset."

From the adjacent chamber came the hum of a hone, where George was putting an edge to his master's battle-axe.

He rejoined them presently, and mentioned one or two occasions whereon he had witnessed successful strife with dragons now defunct. But he was not in a sanguine mood and presently suggested that Sir Jasper should retire.

"What would you wish for breakfast?" inquired the Portreeve.

"Red meat, wheaten bread and honey," replied Pipkin, "and plenty of mead. If we can engage the pest before noon, so much the better; if not, then we must eat again before doing so. Ere the sun goes west, a dragon, being largely nocturnal, is somnolent; but, as the day advances, he attains to his full energy, and he is at his worst and deadliest about the hour of dusk."

"Take this for your comfort," said Pratt's right-hand man. "He is undoubtedly a very old reptile, and though far from infirm—be under no false hope as to that—cannot fairly be called a dragon in his prime. Youth will be served, as we all know."

Thereupon both heroes retired and, despite the tremendous ordeal now before him, Sir Jasper, having said his orisons and committed himself and his fortunes to the Creator, prepared to sleep as soundly as usual.

"Though few knights but hold a lady in their hearts, to clear their eyes and strengthen their sword-arms, yet for my part, I still believe it better to do one's work without such glorious and distracting obligations," he reflected. "Some day, no doubt, I shall love and seek to prolong our line, now depending upon me for its continuation; but plenty of time, plenty of time; and if, meanwhile, destiny wills that I fall with my face to a foe who shall overtax my powers, then no heart is broken save my own."

He slept, and the moon sailed over slumbering Pongley, while from the reed ronds round about arose the croak of a myriad frogs, and in the black Forest of Blore owls shouted their hollow laughter.

II

THE APPOINTMENT FOR RAINBARROW

HAVING MADE a meal worthy of the occasion, Sir Jasper and his squire, declining the assistance offered, set forth in a grey summer morning to reconnoitre the haunts of the enemy and, if possible, encounter him.

Chance willed that they discovered signs within three miles of the hamlet, for immense impressions of the Lavender Dragon's feet suddenly stared up from a marshy bottom, and while George dismounted and measured these vast tridents stamped into the damp soil, out of willow brakes not above a quarter of a mile distant, the mighty creature himself sprang into the air. The sun had now broken through the mists of morning and his roseal beam struck upon the outstretched pinions of the dragon so that they appeared to be wrought of precious stones. They flapped with slow and solemn strokes and propelled the radiant body of the monster at speed not swifter than a heron's flight. Slowly, lazily he rose, until he shrank to the size of a little morning cloud, then diminished until he appeared no greater than a golden pheasant speeding to the comfort of the distant forest.

Sir Jasper's blue eyes were rolling and his tanned cheek flushed with excitement.

"Can such things be!" he cried.

"Evidently," answered George Pipkin, but without enthusiasm.

"Did you observe that he was carrying a human being between his gigantic jaws?"

"I did, Sir Jasper. A big man he bore away; yet the unhappy wretch looked no larger than a hawthorn berry in the beak of a blackbird. But it is true: he is an old—a very old dragon. IBs flight proclaimed him."

"Old in sin—if indeed a dragon can sin," answered Sir Jasper.

They proceeded to the spot whence the monster had risen and found a clearing in a withy bed. The air was fragrant with the scent of lavender and willow wrens made music. The evidences of a victim did not lack, for beside a bundle of withy wands, freshly cut, they saw a frail, wherein the vanished swain had brought his mid-day meal, and a jerkin of leather, which he had evidently thrown off while at work. A dog also, that had fled before the onset of the dragon, slunk out of the willows and crept to them with his tail between his shaking legs.

Instantly knight and squire set their horses' heads in the direction of the monster's flight, and George expressed a hope that the event of the morning, while unfortunate enough for the day labourer, might yet prove satisfactory from the view-point of their own hopes.

"He has now gone to devour his prey," said Pipkin, "and following the meal, after the manner of all such reptiles, he will seek to slumber. His scent is strong and happily not unpleasant. We may presently get upon it and then, tethering our horses, if fortune be with us, creep to him and destroy him under well-directed blows at the junction of the left wing and the shoulder. Only so will such an enormous creature succumb to us. Open fighting would be impossible. His head is adamant and his tail unapproachable, so long as he shall be wide awake. Indeed, though many a knight has ignored the fact to his detriment, the danger centre and point of highest peril is a dragon's tail; and while engaged with his beak and claws, not a few daring spirits have received their quietus from the back blow, which sweeps a man off his horse, stuns him, and renders him impotent and easy game."

"Should you regard this as a large dragon?" asked the younger.

"Quite the largest I have ever seen, or wish to see," replied his squire.

"Let us talk of other things for a while," responded Sir Jasper. "I am disagreeably conscious of having eaten a little too much of the excellent cold beef we enjoyed for breakfast."

"A groaning table often makes a groaning stomach," admitted George; "but think nothing of it. We shall not be called upon to exert ourselves for some hours at the earliest."

Indeed Pipkin was right, and ere they reached the Woods of Blore, Sir Jasper was hungry again. They had brought with them another ample meal, and having discussed it, made cautious sallies round about the forest in search of scent. To the east lay the Red Rocks, a favourite resting place of the dragon; but the sun had long passed the meridian before they found themselves within sight of this rugged and sequestered gorge. For many miles along the confines of the great wood they had ridden and admired the grandeur of such timber as neither remembered to have seen. Gigantic conifers towered above them, with stems that seemed fashioned of bright, pure silver; and overhead their boughs were dark as night, throwing down a dense shadow upon the flower-lit turf beneath.

It was evening before they reached the Valley of the Red Rocks, and the peaks and pinnacles of this impressive spot already glowed as though red hot under a fine sunset. The place was arid, yet beautiful, and the boulders and crags burned in wondrous and dazzling hues of orange and scarlet, amethyst and rose. It seemed that gems studded these precipices and ragged scarps, for they flashed with rainbow colours and answered the signals of the sinking sun. No herb or shrub appeared to adorn the region, yet, as they proceeded, suddenly beneath them extended a wondrous patch of pale, purple inflorescence and the fragrance of lavender rose to their nostrils.

George started with suspicion, and Sir Jasper inhaled the warning odour. Their steeds also sniffed the scent and pawed the earth.

"It comes from an extensive patch of natural flowers yonder," declared the knight, but Pipkin better appreciated the situation.

"Murrain on your flowers," he whispered. "It is the dragon himself!"

And, looking again, both recognised, in the mass of colour spread beneath them, the outlines of the slumbering saurian.

"It is as I hoped," said George. "He is sleeping the sleep of repletion, and we have fortunately come up the wind to him."

They made a detour and presently approached the monster. Taking cover behind great boulders strewed upon the valley bottom, they brought their horses nearer and still nearer, then drew up, dismounted and took stock of the insensible giant. He slept profoundly, and his great sides rose and fell three feet at every breath. From his open nostrils rumbled a not unmusical snoring, somewhat suggestive of the French horn, and round about him wild creatures gambolled without fear. Half a dozen rabbits leapt and danced between his huge front paws, lizards ran over him and birds hopped along the serrated summit of his vast back, lofty as the ridge-tiles of a mansion. There were indications of great age about him, for though of a sweet and wholesome appearance, he was thin and the elaborate architecture of massy ribs that supported his circumference appeared through his integument and coat of mail. His wings were furled, and his enormous eyes covered by heavy and wrinkled lids. Pipkin, in the greatest excitement, directed Sir Jasper how to proceed.

"Lose not a moment," he said, "but draw off to the left, mount your charger, then couch your lance and let him have it, striking where the pinion lies over the shoulder. With weight of man and horse behind the blow, you shall reach his heart and destroy him instantly."

Then, to his indignation and confusion, the knight made chilling answer.

"Not so, friend," he replied. "It shall never be said that Sir Jasper de Pomeroy slew a sleeping foe. No glory attaches to the act of an assassin."

"Odds bodikins!" hissed George. "This is a *dragon,* and when was it ever heard that a dragon demanded to be treated with the rules of chivalry? Would he have wakened you had the case been reversed? Providence has given the tormentor into your hands, and to ask him to fight fair is little better than self-destruction. He couldn't even if he wanted to."

Sir Jasper was, however, obdurate.

"No created thing shall perish in his sleep by hand of mine," he answered. Then he struck his mailed glove upon his shield, lifted his voice and raised such a volume of sound among the echoing cliffs that the Lavender Dragon awoke. Like curtains his eye-lids ascended and revealed two enormous eyes, glorious as fire opals and large as the rose windows in some great cathedral.

"Bless my life!" cried the dragon in good, nervous English. "What have we here?"

"Death, vile reptile!" shouted Sir Jasper, and laying his lance in rest and drawing down his beevor, he spurred his piebald war-horse forward. But the mighty lizard heaved himself on to his feet and so placed his assailant at a great disadvantage. Now horse and man came only to the monster's knees.

"Wait! Wait! Wait!" he said, lifting one gigantic paw. "Let us understand one another. I appreciate your courtesy in rousing me before you laid on. It was done like a true knight and indicates a courage probably only equalled by your mastery of arms. But I, too, am not devoid of fine feeling in these matters. The sun has already set, and as our encounter is likely to be of some duration, I must point out that, in the gloaming, I shall enjoy unfair advantage that I am loath to take. For I can see in the dark by the light of my own eye-balls—a gift denied to you. We may or may not be evenly matched by daylight, but, with the oncoming of darkness, there can be no question that you would suffer a severe handicap, and this must not be."

Struck dumb to hear a primeval dragon speak after so gentlemanly a fashion, the knight and squire reined in their horses and stared upward with open mouths upon the enemy.

"I am perfectly willing to encounter you, if in your judgment the greatest good to the greatest number will be gained thereby," continued the huge creature quietly, "but you, who have proved yourself the flower of chivalry, must not suffer greater disabilities than myself. I am an old dragon now and I never fought for pleasure even in my palmy days; but I still possess prodigious physical powers, and should little like to exercise them, save under conditions as fair to my opponent as myself."

"This is a dark scheme to evade his doom," whispered George Pipkin. "Parley not a moment, but advance upon him. He doesn't want to fight! The man from the withy bed may have upset him."

Sir Jasper, however, hesitated to take this course, and the enemy again addressed them.

"If I may suggest," he said, "let us meet on Rainbarrow an hour after sunrise to-morrow. There you shall find a smooth, broad plateau whereon you and your squire will be able to manoeuvre your gallant steeds; and the spot also affords an ample theatre for your friends to sustain and support you."

"You would seem to be a reasonable adversary," replied Sir Jasper in doubtful tones. "As for me, my purpose has ever been to play the game with every foe, and I like to believe an enemy is inspired by similar principles; but it is beyond belief that a foul, pestiferous and man-eating dragon should thus seek, even in the jaws of death, to make an honest bargain."

"Why?" asked the monster. "Why suppose that I am acting contrary to my steadfast ideals in this affair?"

"Your 'ideals,' foul cockatrice!" cried George. "Have we not this morning seen you fly away with an innocent peasant from the withy beds? Are you not engaged in digesting him at this moment?"

"What credentials and evidence of good faith can you possibly put before me?" continued Sir Jasper. "Consider my position in this matter as well as your own. If I return to the inhabitants of Pongley-in-the-Marsh and inform them that you are engaged to meet me at sunrise on Rainbarrow, what are they likely to say about it? Surely they will flout me and drive me forth with scorn, judging me such another as Sir Rollo Malherbe, who aforetime came among them, learned particulars of your dimensions and recollected an engagement elsewhere. The natives of this district are no fools—indeed, no Yorkshire-man is ever a fool. You see my predicament if I return with what must seem a fable to the Portreeve of Pongley and his neighbours."

The Lavender Dragon lifted an enormous paw to his low but broad forehead.

"A genuine difficulty," he admitted, "though I might summon witnesses—but no. You must, I fear, trust me to keep my word. I attach the utmost importance to truth-telling. Your squire will report the same tale and, if need be, you may exaggerate a trifle without overstepping strict veracity. Behold how night spreads her purple mantle upon the gorge, robbing the rocks and crags of their ruddy splendour; observe how my eyes now shine like glowing meteors and cast a ray of brilliance down the glen. They were far brighter once. But tell the Pongley people how you surprised me on the edge of twilight and that the day was too far spent for our encounter. Do not hesitate to assure them that you credit me; even indicate that I showed a measure of reason, little to have been expected from such a being. Inform Pongley that I shall be upon Rainbarrow at the appointed time, and pray, pray believe me yourself when I tell you so."

Sir Jasper looked up at the huge head from which these words proceeded in a sonorous but educated voice.

Then the dragon, tired of standing, sat down.

"Do you understand the nature of an oath?" inquired the knight.

"I do," replied the monster. "I am not unfamiliar with humanity and have had relations with them quite other than those recorded, to my disfavour, by Pongley and more important places. I appreciate the significance of an oath and am perfectly willing to take one, if that will content you."

"You are no ordinary dragon," declared Sir Jasper. "Such as I have already heard about, conducted themselves in very different fashion, fought with abandon, spewed fire, hit below the belt and pursued their defensive and offensive operations without self-control, civil conversation, or any sense of honour. They have risen from the slime, they have been horrible, formidable and utterly repulsive in every way. Mankind is accustomed to believe that the only possible dragon is a dead one; yet here you sit, within reach of my unconquerable lance, and discourse as fluently and grammatically as myself. Even an oath appears to be within your experience. You are courteous, self-contained, intelligent. Your natural weapons are terrific, and no doubt you know exceedingly well how to use them; but, as you confess, you are no longer young, and, if I mistake not, your hinder claws show evidences of gout."

"Once it was acute," explained the Lavender Dragon. "Now alas! it threatens to become chronic. With acute gout, one throws it off and has good times between the attacks; but once the ailment assumes a chronic form, we are forced much to modify our activities. Do not think, however, that I advance these facts as a reason for evading your attack. Far from it. I am still in the possession of very great activity and may give you at least a run for your money."

Like lamps fed by a rainbow the Lavender Dragon's eyes burned steadily above them.

"It is as though we talked to a lighthouse," murmured George Pipkin.

"In the name of your Maker, then—your Maker and my own—you swear to be on Rainbarrow to-morrow morning, wet or fine," said Sir Jasper; and the dragon lowered his prodigious head with becoming reverence and shut his eyes. The action plunged the party into darkness.

"I will—so help me," declared the great creature. It was a strange interview, even for the Dark Ages, and Sir Jasper began to believe that all must be a dream from which he would presently awaken.

"Have you ever fought with a belted knight before?" inquired the squire, and the dragon confessed that he had.

"Once, and once only," he admitted.

"And seeing that you still live, I suppose—?"

The Lavender Dragon indicated a slight scar among the blue scales on his off fore leg.

"He pricked me and no more. I was younger and far more agile of body in those days than at present. The battle lasted exactly thirty-five seconds."

"You slew him?"

"No. I gave him a good thumping and told him not to do it again. He never did."

"His name?" inquired George briefly.

"Sir Claude Pontifex Fortescue," replied the dragon.

"What befell him?" asked Sir Jasper. "He was before my time, and it is many a long year since he was at court, or in company. There is, however, still some speculation among his own generation as to what became of Sir Claude."

"Little need to inquire farther," growled George Pipkin. "A knight who has been thumped by a dragon, and told not to do it again, would scarcely show his face in the society of his peers."

"That's another story—too long to tell you now," declared the huge creature. "Until to-morrow, then, on Rain-barrow?"

"I trust you—chiefly because I must," replied Sir Jasper. "Do not disgrace yourself, or you will disgrace me. Observe that I treat you as an equal."

"I do, and am flattered accordingly," replied the other. "Fear nothing: I shall be there. And now draw off your steeds, and give me room to spread my wings. I thank you."

He rose upon his four feet, towered above them, resembling, if anything, a cyclopean sofa, and slowly opened his pinions. They creaked a little and he sighed.

"Rheumatism," he said, then sprang aloft with a roar, like a sixty-knot gale of wind, soared away and vanished under the stars.

"And that's the last you'll see of him," prophesied the squire, relief and bitterness strangely mingled in his remark.

"Think better of the fellow," urged Sir Jasper; but George refused to be comforted.

"You have spurned the gifts of Fortune," he answered, "and can hope for no more of her favours."

III

VIGIL

DURING THE long ride back to Pongley, George Pipkin preserved a very unfavourable attitude toward his master.

"When new ideas clash with old," he said, "when age falls back upon experience and youth advances, armed, as usual, with mistaken opinions, then comes the tug-of-war. But there is no place in knight-errantry for these ingenuous ideals, and to pit your mistaken standards of dragon warfare against my proven knowledge was the height of folly, as you will live to learn."

Sir Jasper let him run on, but at length some word from George stung the hero into retort.

"Has this silver-shafted lance been blessed by three bishops and an archbishop, or has it not, Pipkin?" he asked, shaking his majestic spear.

"What of it?" replied the other.

"It has; and that being so, is it a weapon to thrust into anybody while he sleeps? I ask you?"

"The mistake you are making is to treat an atrocious reptile and enemy of man as though he were on the same footing as yourself," replied Pipkin. "Your rules of conduct are all thrown upside down, just because this particular dragon, by some gift of necromancy, can talk and pretend to be a decent member of society. You know perfectly well that he is not. You have his disgusting record. He has devoured men, women and children. He has cast a cloud of horror and dismay upon this neighbourhood for years, and no doubt, before he came here, he carried on after the same fashion somewhere else. A dragon is a dragon. They are all the misbegotten spawn of hell, and we are told to bruise their heads and warned that they shall bruise our heels. By the will of God you had him at your mercy; he was given to you that you might destroy him; but you lost your senses and showed a lamentable confusion of thought, a mistaken code, both of honour and duty, whereof he took full advantage. Now one of two things must happen. Either he won't come to Rainbarrow, or else he will. The betting is all Lombard Street to a crab apple that he doesn't; but if he does, then you may be very sure he knows a great deal more about Rainbarrow than we do, and will not stand your onset unless he has secret advantages that the conflict must too soon reveal."

"'A good thumping,'" mused Sir Jasper. "That is un-knightly language, George."

"Bluff," replied the squire. "He spoke only to pour scorn upon your Order. And now you yourself may cheapen knighthood, which is already at a low rate of discount for various reasons. Fight to-morrow, if you get the chance, as you never fought before; and for the sake of mankind and your own name, let no false ruth or other nonsense stay your steel. A dragon is like a mad dog. We do not encounter such a beast with punctilio, or the courtesies of the tourney. Get him down and out by the swiftest and most sanguinary means within your power. And trust me to help you if half a chance offers."

"You lack imagination," answered the younger and more enlightened adventurer. "You do not apparently see, or feel, George, that we have met a being by many degrees removed from the conventional dragon of history and experience. This beast, had he been created on a more economical plan and less material devoted to his prodigious carcase, might have been amenable to human discipline and even culture. He has a kind face. He is very old. I would even go so far as to say that, of course under other conditions, he might have left the world better than he found it."

"He has left the world lonelier at any rate," replied Pipkin sourly, "but so long as he does leave the world, between six and seven to-morrow morning, I care not. You may set his virtues on his tombstone; but first look to it there shall be a funeral."

George proceeded to expatiate on the technique of fray with dragons and gave Sir Jasper many a valuable hint; yet there was none the less a cloud between them when they drew rein and entered the village. For the knight resented the squire's attitude to their common enemy; while George much feared that the morrow might bring either disgrace from a sceptical country-side, should the dragon play false, or some exhibition of ill-timed clemency, resulting in Sir Jasper's own destruction if the monster did appear.

Nor could their supper serve to calm the agitated nerves of either; for the men and even more the women of Pongley showed a disinclination to believe the extraordinary story they brought back with them from the Red Rocks. A base fellow or two went so far as to sneer and hint that the Portreeve's hospitality was being abused; but Jacob Pratt, with admirable courtesy, silenced the whisperers.

"It will be time to display our feelings to-morrow," he said, "if Rainbarrow is drawn blank. To-night we are not justified in doubting Sir Jasper's word, or the Lavender Dragon's promise. Many strange things happen in the world, and I still hope to see the blood of our foe leap in a ruddy cataract down the steep of the hills after breakfast."

When supper was ended, Sir Jasper got him to the little fane of St. Cormoran, a Yorkshire martyr of old time; and there, with his silver lance and helmet laid before the altar, he kept vigil before battle until the barn cocks crew. Then, at the first shiver of light, when a glimmer as of old ivory widened about the morning star, the spectrum of St. Cormoran himself appeared to Sir Jasper, and the knight beheld the vision of a dignified ancient, clad in grey robe and cowl, and having a snow white beard that descended beneath the rope of his girdle.

The watcher expected some word of cheer and hope, but received no more than practical advice.

"Get off to bed," said the saint. "Snatch a couple of good hours' slumber while there is time, and make a light breakfast. Remarkable experiences await you to-day, and to enter upon them short of sleep is not piety but fool-hardiness."

With that the ghost vanished, and Sir Jasper, whose eyes indeed had long threatened to close, returned to the dwelling of the Portreeve, threw off his garments and was soon unconscious.

Anon George Pipkin aroused him, and whether he would or no, his master partook of a meagre meal as St. Cormoran directed, for there was not time to do otherwise. Already the entire population of Pongley-in-the-Marsh was streaming towards Rainbarrow, where that flat but elevated table of land rose dimly against the morning, and when Sir Jasper and his squire galloped onto the plateau, they were the last to arrive.

The Lavender Dragon, however, had not yet made his appearance, though it now wanted but five minutes of six o'clock.

IV

THE DRAGON KEEPS HIS WORD

ABOUT AN open space, flanked with a forest on one side and sloping by abrupt declivities of thorn and furze upon the other, the inhabitants of Pongley were assembled. The elders of the hamlet stood grouped together, while the lesser folk surrounded the plateau and made an audience for the approaching struggle. Above a thousand souls were gathered there, and they greeted the knight and his squire somewhat coldly as they trotted out upon the arena.

Of the Lavender Dragon as yet appeared no hint, though, from time to time, this or that spectator, pointing to the air, cried that he was on the wing. But while many a delicate cloud, feathered with morning gold, swept westerly upon the wind, not one resolved itself into the foe.

At six o'clock, concealing a growing concern behind the bars of his helmet, Sir Jasper took the field, and the great piebald steed galloped, caracoled and curveted handsomely. He made a noble picture, but the public was not there for horsemanship; the sense of the company

turned against him; hard words flew on Rainbarrow and the knight
began to experience a moral chill under his armour. What if indeed
he stood convicted of an awful error? Among all those present one
only, George Pipkin, knew that his mistake was venial and centred
in a blind trust, where trust had been folly; but the others would
accuse him, and his squire also, of something far worse than cre-
dulity. Indeed, the few who had accepted his narrative now scorned
themselves for doing so, and even the Portreeve's patience began to
break down.

Sir Jasper, with his back to the woods, drew rein and considered
how best to make his peace with a gathering body of opinion very
unfavourable. He was just about to doff his helm and address them,
when the Portreeve and others approached and Jacob Pratt spoke
uncomfortable words.

"Sir Knight," he said, "if knight indeed you are, it is now apparent
that you have played upon the goodwill and trust of well-meaning
and kindly folk. You have lied to us and fooled us, and you are either
a coward or——"

Suddenly a chorus of loud cries stopped the speaker's mouth and
frenzied excitement broke out upon every face.

"Look to yourself! He is there—he is upon you!" screamed the
people, while children shouted and ran to their parents, dogs barked
and bristled, a fragrant scent permeated the morning breeze. In
another moment the immense and roseal beak of the Lavender
Dragon poked suddenly from the coppice, and before Sir Jasper
could defend himself, or George Pipkin aid him, the monster bad
picked up both knight and charger as cleanly, firmly and gently as a
trained retriever grasps a fallen bird.

Sir Jasper and his terrified steed struggled to escape, but the
dragon lifted his head and they were now thirty feet above the
herbage. Then, as the populace fled before him, the gorgeous but
unsportsmanlike foe waddled hugely out upon the turf and spread
his wings. They flashed, as though they had been gigantic Oriental umbrellas of state, and blinded the beholders; while in another

moment the ancient saurian began to rise. Pipkin, with a wild oath, charged and swung Sir Jasper's mace, which he carried until the knight should have need of it; but he did not get to close quarters for, with a swift but sure flick of the tail, his opponent swept squire and steed to the ground in utmost confusion and, before they could return to attack, the Lavender Dragon was on the wing. A few stones and quarterstaves rattled harmlessly against his purple stomach and fell back upon the heads of those who had thrown them; and then the great beast soared upward among the lights of the morning and soon dwindled to a little star amongst the streaming cirri in the blue.

All was over, and the baffled Pipkin, flinging himself again upon the earth, buried his brown face in the sward and wept like a child.

The Portreeve himself sought to comfort George.

"There is only one bright side to this unhappy incident," declared Jacob Pratt. "Your master has been proved a man of his word and a knight without fear or reproach. Had his skill in arms been equal to his nobility of character—however, let that pass. He is not the first hero who has perished in a good cause. We will cherish his memory while regretting his inefficiency. And so home to breakfast, remembering always that God knows best."

But George was not prepared to take this terrible misfortune lying down. Indeed, he rose immediately, dashed the tears from his eyes and declared that in his opinion all was not quite lost.

"I know better concerning the accursed thing than you do," he replied, "and there is more in this rape of a rare knight than meets the eye. The dragon is a traitor, as might have been expected, for never was dragon known who did not fight foul and aid his clumsy and brute strength with cunning tactics and treacherous strategy. But Sir Jasper is not dead. The brute picked up him and his horse with a great deal of care. Neither one nor the other was injured, save morally, and I doubt not they have been conveyed to some secret holt and haunt of the creature, there to be kept alive for its own purposes. It may torture him, starve him and torment him in a thousand ways to make a dragon's holiday; but one thing is certain: it will never fight him. The wretch is no fool, and very well knows that, put to test of open battle against a man of such incomparable powers as my master can display, it would soon be swept to destruction."

"And what do you propose to do?" inquired the Portreeve.

"I propose to make my way through the dark Woods of Blore, to reach the entrance to the Lavender Dragon's domain, to demand entrance, on pain of a punitive expedition, and learn the fate of Sir Jasper though my own life pay forfeit."

All Pongley cheered the squire's determination, and with one accord the people crowded about George, clasped his hand and wished him well.

As the assembly proceeded from Rainbarrow homeward, Pipkin explained that existence without Sir Jasper held scant attraction for him.

"I am not one of those fortunate men," he said, "who is a hero to his wife. My home, to be frank, promises no welcome worth mentioning. A saddle suits me better than my chair in the ingle nook, and I prefer the sound of the winter wind to the voice of my spouse at the best of times. For that matter, they have much in common. In any case, did I return, my own man, with this appalling story, there would be few flags flying for me, I assure you. Therefore, give me a day's provender and I will set forth to the woods and save Sir Jasper, or perish with him."

An hour later the old campaigner galloped off upon his self-appointed task; but he did not depart before uttering a promise to return and relate the facts concerning his master, if it should presently be within his power to do so.

V

THE DRAGON EXPLAINS

AT AN elevation of about a quarter of a mile, the Lavender Dragon pursued his aerial way. Beneath him rustic sons of the morning went forth to their labours and the pastoral life of the plains proceeded. Ahead, in a gloomy band against the western sky, extended the vast woodlands of Blore. Hither came the flying monster on leisurely wings, which flapped with a sound not unmusical, and created that aeolian humming heard by those who have stood beneath telegraph wires in a high wind. The stout horse and his rider in no way encumbered him. An owl thinks less of a fat mouse than the Lavender Dragon thought of the two tons he was now conveying through the air at the rate of forty miles an hour.

But Sir Jasper remained not silent under these indignities.

"False wretch!" he cried. "Is it thus you keep your oath? Was it for this you shut your untruthful eyes at the name of our Creator and swore that you would meet me in a life and death combat upon the crest of Rainbarrow? Accursed above all other dragons shall you be, and infamous in history while man is left upon the earth to read it! Little should I have imagined that dragon could do worse than dragon has already done; but you—you are the vilest, basest progeny of an infamous breed. Your poisonous blood is upon your own head. You are lost; and if I doubted for a moment the outcome of our encounter, I doubt no more. Your fate is sealed, and whether my lance or another's drive you out of life, die you shall at the hand of outraged man, and that probably sooner than you imagine!"

But the Lavender Dragon answered never a word and Sir Jasper, when his natural wrath was a little cooled, found reason assert itself.

It was clear that if his enemy replied, he must open his jaws to do so, in which event the knight suddenly perceived what would happen to him and his charger: they must fall to earth and be miserably and unromantically destroyed. But both were destined for another fate, and retreating into the tumultuous cavern of his own thoughts, Sir Jasper began to consider what might be expected to happen next. He felt tolerably sure that the dragon dared not now encounter him in fair fight; but would it presently be possible to force a battle? He hoped so, yet felt little certainty. The saurian had proved as artful as he was old, and his victim doubted not that, when again they came to earth, it must be under conditions where little opportunity offered to his right arm and silver lance. He was wrong again, however, for after flying above the black pines of Blore for a league or thereabout, the dragon abated his speed and hovered over a clearing, where the little blossoms of wood strawberry, cyclamen and lady's slipper made a jewelly carpet amid the silver pillars of the forest. Gently the monster volplaned down into this sequestered glen and opened his jaws to liberate the captives.

"Compose yourself," said the Lavender Dragon as soon as his mouth was free to speak. "Tidy your attire, doff your helm, suffer your charger to crop a little of this excellent pasture and listen to me. You are naturally annoyed; I have put you into a position destructive of knightly dignity; I have struck confusion into those exalted ideals by which you rule your conduct; but one story is only good until we have heard the other. I know exactly how you are feeling and I am well aware that my dragon's blood is about the only thing that you suppose can wash out the extraordinary affront this day has put upon you. Sir Jasper, you shall have it—a pint, a quart, a flagon, a tierce, a barrel—but not until you have listened to what I am about to relate.

"I heard your remarks while we were on the wing," he continued, "and I sympathise fully with your fury and indignation. You could hardly have said less; but in one particular your memory failed you and you were unjust to me. I never asserted that I would fight you on Rainbarrow. I distinctly swore that I would 'meet' you there. I am a truthful dragon and I chose my words and kept my oath. But let this pass. It is enough that I promise you full and complete satisfaction at a future date. Indeed, if you are still in a mind to it, to-day, before the sun goes down, you shall seek to destroy me without any unfair conditions whatsoever. A squire shall be furnished, and if your attractive war horse is rendered less formidable and agile than usual by the events of the morning, you may have your choice of a dozen other splendid chargers as fine as he, all fresh and ready for the field."

"I fall on at once without further parley," declared Sir Jasper. "I am a man of deeds, not words, and nothing you can possibly say will wipe this stain off my scutcheon. Only your own base heart's blood may do it."

"To fight before I have spoken would not suit me," answered the other in a calm but resolute voice. "Sit here, cool your fiery forehead with a dock leaf and listen a little longer. Do not imagine that you are in my hands. On the contrary, I am in yours. I, too, believe that deeds speak louder than words, as I hope to show you by noonday. But first I insist upon it that you listen to me, and I give you my word, as a lover of truth, that you shall not listen in vain."

With ill grace the young man flung himself upon the turf, and for a moment there was no sound but the steady cropping of his philosophic horse, whose custom was to gather his few rose buds when and where he might. Then the Lavender Dragon, assuming a recumbent attitude, proceeded in this curious fashion.

"Even as the world itself was hatched from the Mundane Egg made by our Creator, as the Phoenicians and Egyptians rightly maintain, so all primitive orders of living things likewise emerged to life in that manner. Dragons are among the most ancient of created beings, and they have unfortunately, though not, I fear, undeservedly, personified evil from the earliest times of man. Nowadays we dragons stand as the symbol of Sin in general and paganism in particular. Satan has been termed the Great Dragon; it is declared that the saints shall trample the dragon under their feet. Mankind has also confused the dragon with chieftainship; hence Pen-dragons—leaders, or kings, created in times of peril. Since Apollo destroyed Python there has reigned enmity between my species and all gods and men who stood for righteousness; and therefore you will judge of my personal astonishment when I came to years of understanding and found myself, not only on the side of the angels from the first, but also entirely opposed to the principles and practice of my own race. In fact a dragon with a conscience—a freak of our common Mother, a caprice of Nature! My great-uncle was the celebrated Dragon of Wantley, in this county; and when he found that I entertained opinions subversive of our family interests and desired, if possible, to heal the breach established in primal time between our kindred and the children of men, he disowned me with fury, beat me cruelly, for I was then a mere dracunculus, and cast me out. My parents were already dead, and I wandered friendless for some three centuries. Then my great-uncle perished under the sword and spear of More of More Hall, a very notable knight, and elsewhere, at other times and seasons, our dwindling race was decimated by yours as history records.

"Among famous dragon-slayers—of whom St. George, that beheaded the far-famed Green Dragon of Syria, stands first—are numbered St. Philip, the Apostle, who accounted for the terror of Phrygia; St. Martha, who with unexampled courage destroyed Terasque, the Scourge of Aix; St. Florent, who slew an ancestor of my own upon the Loire; while St. Cado and St. Maudel of Brittany, and St. Keyne of Cornwall also played havoc with our clan. St. Michael and St. Margaret, Pope Sylvester and the Archbishop of Dol, Denatus and St. Clement of Metz—all these eminent persons succeeded against us; and La Gorgouille, a very formidable and gigantic dragon, responsible for much evil on the banks of Seine, fell at an advanced age to the gallant St. Romain of Rouen.

"Thus we have gone down fighting to the last, and now, as I think, not above half a dozen of us shall be found in civilisation, though a few still remain beyond its borders concealed amid the sandy antres of Africa and the frozen forests of the North. For my part, all endeavours to make the world of men perceive that I desired their friendship failed. Nor do I blame anybody. Centuries of antagonism, suspicion and hatred cannot be destroyed by an individual no matter how great his goodwill. I went my way, found the Woods of Blore, established my seat therein and anon encountered a lady dragon, orphaned under the usual circumstances, and alone and friendless as myself.

"We loved at first sight and contracted an alliance; but hardly had I erected a noble home and built for my wife a fortified palace and castle worthy of her, when she left me—I hope and believe for a better world. She shared my opinions and was of a tender and gentle disposition. She threw herself into my pursuits, learned the human language of the country, which I had been at pains to master, and strove unavailingly to create some golden bridge of understanding by which we could approach man in friendship for our common advantage. But, needless to say, she failed, and it was as a result of wounds, won in a frantic but futile attempt to charm a body of crossbow men upon the march, that she lost her beautiful life.

"Anon you shall see her grave in the centre of our public park at Dragonsville. For to my city I am about to convey you, Sir Jasper; and if, after you have inspected it, consulted those who inhabit it, and heard and seen such as bestow upon me their affection and regard—if, I say, after that experience, you still desire to fight with me and lay me low, upon my honour you shall be granted every opportunity to do so.

"What remains to be said you must learn at a later time; but now, if you are rested, we will proceed and be at home for luncheon. I am a grass-eater like your noble charger, and doubtless some fine bales of sweet clover hay await us both; but for you is already served such a banquet as we are happy to prepare for a noble and welcome guest."

"They are then expecting us?" inquired the knight, and the Lavender Dragon admitted that it was so.

"I confess to my little plot," he said. "I was quite determined that you should enjoy wider knowledge of me and my ways before you attempted, perhaps successfully, to destroy me. A thing once done cannot be undone, Sir Jasper, and if by chance, in future time, you had learned the truth, I am bold to believe that remorse might have darkened your soul and unavailing regrets cast a shadow on your unstained career."

With that the dragon, tenderly picking up his new acquaintance and the piebald horse, ascended once more into the empyrean. They proceeded for a matter of twenty miles over the bosky gloom of the forest and then the scene changed, a fair and sun-kissed vale opened beneath them and, girdled by a mighty wall, Sir Jasper perceived what men of a later time would have described as a remarkably large and distinguished garden city, watered by a sparkling river.

Wide, open spaces, adorned with lakes and fountains, noble trees and blazing passages of flower colour spread between human dwellings. These stood in the shape of a star whose points extended to all quarters of the compass. The houses were solidly built of stone, and their roofs, of red and sunbaked tiles, seen from this elevation, presented a design of considerable charm. In the midst rose a gigantic castle of barbaric architecture—a place so hugely planned, with doors so vast and towers so lofty, that the Lavender Dragon himself might move and dwell with comfort and elegance therein. It was his home, and upon an immense terrace before the southern front he now descended.

Nor was there none to welcome him. To the amazement of Sir Jasper, half a hundred stalwart men, in the livery of the Lavender Dragon, greeted the monster as he alighted. Their faces shone with well-being and they crowded about him, cheered him, saluted the visitor with courtesy and friendship and led away his agitated horse. Others took his spear and sword; while an old and kindly retainer begged that he would follow him, where he might rest, refresh, doff his armour and presently partake of the banquet already prepared in his honour.

"I will see you anon," said the Lavender Dragon. "This is Nicholas Warrender, my seneschal. You will be happy with him and a company of our comrades until the afternoon. For the moment I want my dinner before all else."

The dragon led the way into his castle and settled himself with a mighty sigh before six huge trusses of sweet-smelling hay in his own dining-room—a chamber about twice as large as the cathedral of

St. Paul. But Nicholas Warrender proceeding with Sir Jasper, conveyed him to an apartment, huge enough, yet not uncomfortably spacious, and there left him to make his toilet and choose from half a hundred comely garments what he would best like to put on.

Arrayed at length in a doublet of grey velvet with amber slashings, comfortable grey hose and a collar of delicate lawn, the knight struck a bell upon his table and Nicholas returned. He led the dragon's guest into an apartment where some two hundred men and women already awaited him, and the seneschal introduced Sir Jasper to a dozen of the party, who welcomed him with much friendship and good cheer. They were for the most part elderly; but age sat lightly about them and the guest could not fail to note that in their faces one saw no lines of care, no haggard tell-tale stamp of sorrow hidden, or tribulation concealed. Here was happiness—not simulation of the thing, proper to all well-bred and tactful companies meeting together about some common business of council or entertainment, but the genuine emotion; and furthermore he felt amost embarrassed by the manner of their greeting, for their one concern was his own comfort and pleasure. They vied with each other in warmth of welcome; they revealed nothing concerning themselves, but displayed only an altruistic regard for his satisfaction in every particular.

"Ladies and gentlemen," he said, "would you kill me with kindness?"

"Kindness never kills," declared Nicholas Warrender. "Kindness, Sir Knight, is the small change of a good heart, given to all who extend a hand for it, and as gladly to be received as given. Kindness, in fact, makes our wheels go round, and if it became a human habit—— However, we are not here to preach, but eat. These lampreys come from our own river and are worthy of your attention."

After the meal Sir Jasper was introduced to a great number of men and women; and others of a younger generation also entered, that they might see and speak with him. If the elders were cheerful with the light of contentment upon their faces, how much more did the same radiance illuminate the young! Maids and boys appeared equally joyous. They greeted the guest with an ingenuous delight and respect, which Sir Jasper was well qualified to appreciate, and in the shy friendship of these young people he swiftly found an exquisite pleasure. They, too, according to their ages and predilections, offered him what they themselves most appreciated. The girls begged him to come and dance with them, or hear them sing; the boys, heedless that he had just dined after a trying journey, hoped that he would join their games and suffer them to teach him new and ravishing pastimes.

Then happened a strange thing, for among those introduced to his notice, Sir Jasper heard many names not unfamiliar.

"This," said the seneschal, "is Thomas Fagg, the woodcutter, and our friend with the dusty face is good Master Hobanob, who helps to bake our bread. Here stands Nicol Prance, once on a time a master-thatcher, but in Dragonsville the houses are all tiled, so he has learned a new trade. This is our oldest inhabitant—of course after L.D. himself—Johnny Cobley, aged ninety-five, once a swineherd, now enjoying his old age and the object of our special care. Here you see Mistress Avisa Snell, and Ann, her daughter, promised in marriage to Billy Greg, the keeper of the fountains. This pretty maid is Mary Fern, who lost her man in the wars and was just going—silly soul—to take her beautiful and useful life, when L.D. found her and brought her amongst us. Betsy Snow and Jenifer Mardell are towers of strength when good plain sewing is to be done; and here is our last arrival before your honoured self. Come forward, Abram Archer, and salute Sir Jasper."

The withy-cutter, last seen in the jaws of the dragon, stepped from the throng. He looked still a little dazed, as a man who has just emerged from a dream; but he was laughing and evidently well pleased to find himself among so many old friends in this flourishing settlement.

"I bring these good people to your notice," proceeded Nicholas Warrender, "because they are all Pongley-in-the-Marsh folk, and you may by chance have heard their names."

"I heard that they had all been devoured by the Lavender Dragon," answered Sir Jasper, and his remark awakened hearty merriment.

"We come here to eat, not to be eaten," said Hugh Hobanob; "for what is Dragonsville but a glorified Pongley after all?"

"A Pongley where there is happiness rather than anxiety, health instead of sickness, abundance in place of scarcity," added the seneschal. "Here we work, but never for ourselves. Note that. Perceive, for instance, our gardens. I will show them to you."

The company stepped into the air and many walked beside Sir Jasper as he accompanied his guide.

"We are great gardeners," continued the seneschal. "Yet nobody ever does a day's work in his own. Everybody applies his best energies and skill to the garden of somebody else. To cultivate your garden is very good, and we are well advised to do so, but how much better to cultivate the garden of your neighbour! It is, in fact, one of our greatest delights to create horticultural surprises for our friends."

"Surely confusion might arise and disappointment, since tastes differ on this subject as on every other," suggested the knight.

"Confusion does arise," admitted Nicholas. "Thus he who hoped for radishes may find a superfluity of turnips in his garth; while the lover of kale is snowed under with endive, or spring onions. But what of it? Nothing results save cheerful laughter, and never was a better joke than when Jane Blee, who is devoted to the carrot and parsnip, discovered her garden patch obliterated under tansy and alkanet. Even L.D., who sees a joke with utmost difficulty, laughed long at Jane. But what did she do? Why, seek the gardens of her neighbours and help herself to all that she desired. For our good things are in common and our chief delight is to give of our best where it will be most appreciated. This principle runs through all our rule of living. It actuates old and young; it is the mainspring of Dragonsville: hence the brightness of our faces and the heartiness of our laughter."

"And what is the underlying impulse of this curious vagary?" inquired the visitor. "How call you this spirit which accounts for your well doing and well being?"

"For particulars you must listen to L.D.," replied the grey-beard. "And when I say 'L.D.,' think it no term of undue familiarity, or disrespect. Thus we all speak of the Lavender Dragon, both behind and before his face. It was his own idea, for we were desirous of a more respectable and sonorous title. Indeed we offered him a crown once, and on that occasion he did indeed laugh—so riotously that he blew down a score of houses and devastated several acres of his own favourite food—I mean kidney beans. But he declined the diadem; he would not even accept the office of President. 'I am,' said our dragon, 'just "L.D." to all of you, no more, no less. Your friend, so long as you will permit it, your well-wisher and your companion in this arduous business of living out the years of our lives with dignity, energy and common advantage.'"

"And tell me of Lilian Lovenot," begged Sir Jasper. "She, too, was a Pongley maiden, and I assure you that her disappearance caused much bitter feeling, for she was loved and cherished and held the pride and top flower of all the hamlet."

The seneschal's face fell.

"It may be so. L.D. rarely errs; but it is true that once, or perhaps twice, he has brought among us those who showed an inclination to return whence they came. His rule, however, is to seek out only the lonely, the sad, the failures, the care-worn and life-stained people, or the young who are unwanted and unloved—all such as have only heard of happiness."

"Hence his predilection for orphans, no doubt," murmured Sir Jasper.

"Exactly. In the case of Lilian, L.D. judged that she would be happier here, because, among us, are not a few of her own standing and rank. For he was aware that the Lovenots were no parents of hers. He thought, therefore, of her own happiness, and I fear rather overlooked the pleasure she already gave to others—a singular lapse from his own standards. Pongley's loss was, however, Lilian's gain. She is exceedingly joyous at present, lives in the Castle and ministers no little to L.D.'s own content; for, while the bulk of us are only concerned to make each other happy, and so indirectly please the master of Dragonsville, a few of the more learned and cultured—such as can speak wisely, or sing harmoniously—spend a measure of their time with him. He delights in music and story-telling, and his chief material pleasure is to sit in the great central fountain and let the jet beat down upon him as it falls. This is not always good for him, however. He is much afflicted with gout, and the distemper will carry him off some day. These fields on our right are entirely devoted to growing Colchicum Autumnale, a crocus of the fall, from whose roots and seeds our doctor compounds the medicine to lessen L.D.'s sufferings."

They sauntered through the little, cobbled streets presently, where folk were busy about their affairs.

"We are, of course, a pastoral people," explained the seneschal, "but there is a certain amount of industrial activity among us also and we are self-supporting in every way. We grow our herds, weave and spin our wool, delve into the earth for iron and make of it our needful implements. Life is simple here, because the need for money does not exist; and even if it did, to save were impossible by reason of the law that directs and controls everything. 'Giving,' is the watch-word here, and 'getting' conveys no impression to the rising generation; while, to us elders, this business of 'getting' merely signifies that reactionary and unsocial process which keeps the outer world so short of the content and happiness we enjoy. But hither comes the merry man of the castle. L.D. is probably anxious to see you and sends his messenger."

It was so, and Sir Jasper learned from a jester, who now approached, that his presence in the great Hall of Reception would be welcome.

The buffoon was by no means as cheerful as many of his companions; but only a facial accident explained his apparent depression. He was a dry bird, by the name of Dicky Gollop, and he explained to Sir Jasper how, on an occasion of hawking with his former master, he had made a jest which the baron, who owned him, took in bad part.

"Before I could explain my point," said Dicky, "the dull old dog alighted from his horse, directed a dozen varlets to pinion me against a tree, then beat me with the flat face of his sword until I lost consciousness. There he left me, still crucified to the pine, and there I must have perished but for L.D., who, passing that way, saved the situation. I regained my understanding in Dragonsville and rejoiced to abide here. I have but one daily regret, and honestly I believe that I am the only member of the community who regrets anything at all."

"What may that be?" enquired Sir Jasper.

"My inability to strike the right note of humour for L.D.," replied Dicky Gollop. "It is not my fault, for I really can be funny when in good form. Others will tell you of my jokes and quips, my quirks and quiddities. I am an excellent wag and make men, and even women, lose themselves in hurricanes of laughter. My repartee is rapier-like, my badinage bewilders with its lightning flashes. For a *jeu de mot,* a quibble, a conundrum, or a double entendre, there is nobody to approach me, and yet I lack the power to make my revered master enjoy the luxury of a hearty roar."

"Perhaps that is as well from all I hear," replied the knight; but Dicky would not allow it.

"No, my mission, so far as he is concerned, is a failure. And he knows it. He is as sorry for me as I am for myself. He tries to make me happy by laughing at my jocularity; but jesters are not deceived. Nobody knows quicker than tomfool if his tomfoolery is touching the spot; and in the ordinary high-class establishments, where jesters form part of the retinue, if we don't give our employers sore sides, we soon receive them. But L.D. never shows any impatience at my failure. He observes that I entertain other people, and since the happiness of others is the only thing he cares a brass button about, in this vicarious sense I please him too. As a man, therefore, I am content; as an artist I shall ever harbour a sense of disappointment."

But Dicky's trouble did not interest Sir Jasper. He was himself devoid of humour, and he could not find it in his heart to blame the Lavender Dragon's indifference.

"Many," he said, "derive no great entertainment from the glib tongues and often questionable drolleries of your class. If you do not actually irritate your master, you should be content."

"You are not an artist then," ventured Dicky.

"No," replied Sir Jasper. "I am a serious man engaged in making the world better than I find it."

"To be merrier is also to be better," declared the mirth-provoker. "Man is the only laughing animal, and laughter is too little respected. Every child should be taught to laugh—like a gentleman; since there are horrid forms of laughter, which might be cured in youth, but not afterwards. Those who help the world to laugh, Sir Knight, are worthy of respect as great as the mighty ones, and the lovers of bloodshed and battle, who help it to cry. At least that is L.D.'s opinion, and I shall make him laugh yet if I break my heart a-trying."

With that they entered the draconian presence together.

VI

THE DRAGON GOES ON EXPLAINING

SIR JASPER'S host reclined amid a chaos of woollen cushions each as large as a haystack. They were coloured amber and blue, jade green and orange. Thus they chimed pleasantly with the rose and delicate shades of lilac which played in sparkling iridescence over the vast body of the Lavender Dragon. He had eaten his hay and was now toying with a little mountain of sugared kidney beans piled up upon a plate of gold, while beside it stood an enormous silver goblet, containing fifty gallons of cider.

A girl sat on an ivory chair beside L.D.; and when the knight appeared, she put her little hand on the dragon's paw as he extended his mighty claws to the sweetmeats in the golden dish.

"No," she said, "you must not eat any more. They are horribly bad for you, and you know that Doctor Doncaster has told you these sugared beans should be taken far more sparingly."

The dragon drew back his paw.

"Let me present Sir Jasper de Pomeroy, my dear Lilian," he said, and then turned to the visitor.

"This is Mistress Lilian Lovenot—so to call her. But she and I have reason to think that her real name is otherwise. However, time will show."

The knight bowed and the lady curtseyed, and while they became acquainted, L.D. stealthily helped himself to some more beans. Indeed he tossed a peck into his mighty mouth and munched them quickly, his opal eyes on Lilian.

She was a fair maiden with rich, auburn locks, braided into two heavy bands that descended below her knees. She wore cloth of gold, that fitted close to her sturdy but beautifully modelled body; and the bright fabric was ornamented with emeralds only. Her face was strangely beautiful and winsome, and when her lips parted in a smile, a dimple of the most distracting charm twinkled upon her left cheek. Her eyes especially fascinated Sir Jasper, for they were in lustre and colour like aquamarines.

She spoke in a soprano voice and gave him her hand, which he kissed with courtly respect. They made a striking pair and the dragon gazed upon them benevolently; but he presently interrupted their discourse and bade Lilian leave him with his visitor.

"Depart, dear chuck," he said. "You shall become better acquainted with Sir Jasper anon; for the present he listens to me, and we have some ground to traverse. All that I must say cannot be spoken at a sitting, but if he is so disposed, we will make a beginning this afternoon."

The maiden turned to the knight.

"Do not let him eat too many beans, or drink too much cider," she said. And then she departed, while Sir Jasper had leisure to note the grace of her deportment and progression.

"A blessed girl," said the dragon after Lilian had disappeared. "Beautiful both without, as you perceive, and within, as you shall find. Of her and her mystery more at another time. Now I will proceed with my own story where I left off this morning. When my dear wife died, a great darkness descended upon me and for the space of five-and-twenty years life held no interest or consolation. Do you see yonder mound beside the fountain—the tumulus bowered in hawthorns?"

He pointed out of a lofty window, where shone brilliant displays of blossom, crimson and white, upon a little hill. Sir Jasper nodded.

"There she lies, and there, ere long, I shall lie beside her," said L.D. He heaved a sigh, like the breath of a sinking storm, and one or two tears, each representing a quart of the purest lavender water, splashed upon the cushions.

"Pardon me," said the dragon. He then cleared his throat and proceeded.

"I even contemplated self-slaughter during the full brunt of my bereavement, but a moderate intellect and a good conscience came to my aid. I strove to create fresh interests and immerse myself in such enterprises as should justify existence and be an excuse for my long life. And then I made the astounding discovery that has taken shape in this little republic. I found that the only happiness worthy of being so called is that which we are able to bring to other creatures; and since my own race was beyond the reach of my ambitions in this direction, I turned attention to man—to Homo Sapiens, as he so humorously calls himself—and studied him with immense application for two whole centuries.

"Man, Sir Jasper, viewed as it were from the outside, is a difficult customer, and I was more than once minded to abandon my studies in despair; but I persisted and at length arrived at some general conclusions concerning him. What did I find? I discovered, first, that the thing your species chiefly lacked was humility. Man is far the vainest of created things, and his gift of reason, instead of balancing this defect, and helping him to see himself in a juster perspective with regard to his place in the cosmos, tends as a rule to increase his unfortunate arrogance and insensate pride. Rather than employ his wonderful wits to fathom and accept Nature's law of life, he abuses his best gift, reason, and behaves in a way to put himself below lesser creatures that lack it. Nothing in the world that goes on two feet, or four, or six—that swims, walks, or flies—is ridiculous and immodest save only mankind; and everything that is unseemly and unworthy on earth arises from him alone. Yet he vaunts himself as a being supreme and in a category apart, for ever denying the one touch of Nature that should make our whole world kin. Man, in fact, is far too pleased with himself and, bogged in his inordinate vanity, fails to make the progress that Nature has a right to expect from him. He is falling behind her time-table; he is loitering by the way to admire his own features in every pool; his values and opinions, his hopes and fears, his interests and activities are all far too elementary for his age."

The Lavender Dragon gulped a gallon of cider and proceeded.

"And why has he not travelled further on his appointed road? The answer is a melancholy one. He has doubled back upon his own high-water mark; his tides actually ebb rather than flow. The world contains evidence of a higher civilisation and worthier humanity than exist in it at this moment; for man has fouled the lustral waters of his reason and substituted for pure thinking and higher principles, a degraded and reactionary rule of conduct founded on superstitions so gross that even a simple dragon like myself, coming to their examination with unbiased mind, stands aghast before such a retrograde era.

"It is summed up in an aphorism, my friend. Faith took the wrong turning; Faith—that vital principle of progress—instead of founding her vanes upon the rock of reason and building on those mighty foundations laid by your ancient thinkers, sought otherwhere for her inspiration, set back the clock and lost many centuries by so doing. How much more time your race will be content to squander, I cannot say; how, many more generations of you will still grope in the night of superstition and suffer it to discolour your thought and retard your progress I know not. Only by persisting in your vanity and by blinding yourselves and your children can it be done.

"Your rights and wrongs are all your concern, never your obligations and errors. You are the most ungrateful of created things, and even that dim sense of gratitude, lying in hope of favours to come and represented by early man's first prayer to beings greater than himself—even that was soon lost. Your religion, that might have been a fair and reasonable addition to life, became foul and more foul, because it sprang from fear instead of love, from suspicion instead of trust; and the poison that polluted its beginnings is with it yet. But given loyalty to the laws that made you, and reverence for the things you might become, rather than foolish pride in the things that you are, then the spectacle you present should lead to impatience instead of self-satisfaction, and create a great will and purpose to give reason a chance, that you may learn whereto she is willing to lead you."

Sir Jasper concealed a yawn, for these affairs did not interest him at all. He tried a sugared bean, but found it far too tough a matter for his teeth.

"A few words more and we will proceed from theory to practice," said L.D. "I say, then, that if man but grasped how much he owed to Nature, how little to his own ill-used gifts, he would be more disposed to humility, more inclined to develop his immense static possibilities in dynamic action. What you have done, and are still busily engaged in doing, is merely to postpone what you might do and should do. You shudder at the base instincts you discover—in your neighbours; you blame your primitive ancestors for these savage survivals; but when distinction, altruism and greatness appear, you give no praise to Nature then. No, you praise your noble selves and take all the credit. But I am boring you?"

"Far from it," replied Sir Jasper. "I hate conceit. We are vain popinjays no doubt."

"Possibly you do not live long enough to be otherwise," reflected the dragon. "Your lives are too brief to attain the long view and the balanced vision which I, for example, enjoy. You are still children for a quarter of existence, and often for the whole of it. But you will be more interested in the results of my discoveries. Briefly, our little community and township is the result. I began, in quite a small way, with half a dozen old and disconsolate people, who knew but too well their room was more wanted than their company. One by one I snapped them up and conveyed them hither. I explained my idea

and put it into practice by devoting myself to the pleasure and satisfaction of these lonely individuals. They supplied me with the names
of others, and were in a position to assure me that I should wrong
nobody by increasing my collection. They also declared that amid the
superfluity of children, I might, without causing inconvenience, help
myself as generously as I pleased; and this fact gave me particular
satisfaction, for it is the children I was after. Comparatively little can
be done for the aged, and even middle-aged, but make them comfortable and fairly contented. Their minds are set and they repose
upon a body of fossil opinions, rather than seek the adventure of
new ideas. But how different with youth! The present population of
Dragonsville, save certain notable exceptions, was generally caught
young; and the result has been that my theories, such as they are, win
their opportunity. You must, of course, prove for yourself whether
the results satisfy you. It is possible that you stand on other ground
and mistrust reason; but be that as it may, you will please understand
that this little experiment is conducted on lines of reason alone."

"I saw a very nice church, however," murmured Sir Jasper.

"It is a very nice church. I am coming to that," replied the dragon.
"But first a few more general precepts. Success has nearly always
attended my transplantations. Men and women, removed from the
anxieties and perils of modern civilisation, soon find a new sense of
security growing within them and come to discover that the simplicity of this self-supporting state is worth the loss of much that the
greater world can promise. For the greater world, as you may already
be aware, promises so much and performs so little. The promisers
are among the mighty of the earth, but the performers for the most
go unrecognised and unrewarded. Here we do not promise much,
yet surprise ourselves daily by the beauty of our modest achieve-
ment, and that without stifling the unconquerable spirit of hope,
which enables humanity to keep going, in face of so many temptations to stop going. These temptations arise from man's own false
values and acquired defects of superstition and selfishness, and that
most dreadful of all disabilities known as patriotism. But without,
I say, quenching hope, I yet seek to modify that illusory quality of

the human mind and re-establish it upon surer ground. The result is patience and a growing conviction that things won't happen because we want them to do so, or think that they should happen. The prayer to pray, Sir Jasper, is the prayer you can answer yourself, and the way to pray it is upon your feet, not your knees. This, however, shocks you. I see it in your face."

"I am not sure that I understand," pleaded the knight.

"You should do so, for it is your own rule and ordinance. You held me better dead this morning; but I am sure you did not pray for my destruction: you set out with sword and lance to compass it."

"Let us not return to that," begged the other.

"You may still think it best, when you have heard and seen all. I am at your service as you know. But 'hope'—I was speaking of this great faculty. Hope may simply breed restlessness, and so destroy a man's present content and mar enjoyment of what he has for desire of what he has not. Again hope, which after all is a sort of dreaming, may prevent a man from what he can do, for thinking on what he would like to do. Your Guilds illustrate this inconvenience, for I observe when wages interest the workman so much more than his work, that both work and wages suffer, to the disappointment of everybody concerned."

"You cannot banish hope from the human heart," declared Sir Jasper.

"I would as soon banish sunshine from the earth," replied his companion. "Hope is of the essence of progress. Hope is a precious adjunct of all reason. But the really hopeful thing about your lives is manifest in a great fact that you have yet to grasp. The very gold mine and treasury of human hope, confounding your pessimists and people with weak knees and little faith in your own destiny, lies in this: that reason, like everything else, is subject to change, and that the change, despite occasional and enormous relapses, none the less makes steady progress in well-doing. Reason's natural growth and motion is upward, not downward; forward, not backward; and they who flout reason terribly err, because they will not permit her to do that vital work which lies within her power. At present you are on the crest of a receding wave and far beneath the high-water mark that earlier generations of men have attained; but despair not: the tide is coming in, because it is a part of the great order of things that it should do so. You must judge what man can do by the best that he has done, not from the worst; you must admit that the best can be bettered, and you must turn your faces to the dawn, rather than bury your noses in night and cry that the darkness thickens. You cannot stand still, and while men slip back, man goes onward under the impulsion of reason, that makes for righteousness despite the cross-currents of greed and superstition, vice and folly that seem to hide the fact. Herein lies the most valuable function of hope: to trust man and to trust his future."

"And, meanwhile, what must we do?" asked Sir Jasper.

"Be humble," replied the Lavender Dragon, "and instead of seeking supernatural guides, bend your glances to earth and learn that creatures far beneath you in the scale of existence can teach you exactly those things you most need to know. Instead of demanding assistance from higher beings, whose purpose is obscure, whose friendship is doubtful, whose very existence is merely a matter of opinion, how far better to turn attention upon humble fellow creatures, whose manners and customs are plain to be observed and whose lives command our admiration. Note yonder swarm of bees collecting in the foliage upon my wife's tomb. The unconscious altruism of the honeybee, who does with her might what best becomes her during the short weeks of her existence, is an example so lofty that if it were practised by man the face of this world would be entirely changed. You, my friend, have an ambition to leave the earth sweeter and richer than you find it; and that is exactly what the bee achieves in her own sphere, and what I strive to accomplish in mine. And where reason rules, such an ambition reacts most favourably upon those who persist therein. For it is the solvent of selfishness, the test and touchstone of character. As time passes and the emotion becomes a part of yourself, humility appears; you are emptied of any love for fame, power or pelf; room for happiness is created, and you find, in a negation of personal good, the truest happiness that man may enjoy;

for only by individual self-denial can the sum total of happiness be increased. Such a protagonist is on the right road to justify his own existence and help the flowing tide to new high levels, as yet beyond the reach, but not beyond the hope of reason."

"And how does it work?" inquired the knight, whereupon his host drained his vast beaker and made answer.

"My own modest experience appears to work well; but, of course, it is difficult to be sure if I am really in the right road. You might guess that, where everybody strives to be gracious and useful to everybody else, a condition so unusual in human intercourse would have cast the whole enterprise into confusion; but it is not so. The people are happy and we progress in amenities of life. We live and let live; consequently we live and learn. Without a doubt we are going ahead and getting cleverer in the art of a justified and dignified existence. And the people are happy; because if they were not so, none would stop in Dragonsville. But they remain, though under no compulsion to do so; they assure me that such a life as this meets their requirements and is well worth living."

"They never desert you?"

"Never—hence doubtless the general suspicion at Pongley, and many other places, that I devour them. Once only did a very good man—a holy clerk—declare a desire to return to his grot in the hills. He was a minister of the Christian faith, and having failed to succeed and win his flock as a parish priest, became a hermit and communed in secret with his Maker, living meantime in a natural cavern upon the fruits of the earth. I snapped up Father Lazarus at his own matin prayers, brought him here and talked to him as I have talked to you. He was much annoyed at first, but soon calmed down and enjoyed our home comforts for a season. Then he showed uneasiness and a desire to return to the desert. Presently, however—thanks to his fellow men and women, not to me—he changed his mind, on the condition that I would build him a place wherein he might worship his God and advance the happiness of those who shared his religious opinions.

"I willingly agreed, for you must understand that I am no propagandist, but welcome any ideas which directly or indirectly advance happiness. Upon one point only was I definite. But that's another story and shall be told you at another time. Father Lazarus is a most excellent and high-minded priest, and we are close friends. The people respect him, and it is his custom to seek me on the first day of every month and devote a morning to my personal welfare. He much desires to convert me to his own predilections in the matter of religion; and since the effort is a part of his duty and gives him satisfaction, I always make leisure to attend his discourses."

"You marry and are given in marriage?"

"Certainly. Father Lazarus has celebrated many alliances, and the occasion of a marriage is always a day of rejoicing. I hope you may see such ceremonies. Our children will be a delight to you—if you are fond of children."

"And now a delicate question," ventured Sir Jasper. "All you have told me, Sir Dragon, is of deep interest and instruction; but it is my habit of mind ever to look forward. What of the future of your colony? You, I take it, are but mortal, and cannot live for ever."

"The future," replied L.D., "must look after itself—as it always has done and always will do. I have never been one to bother my brains about anything but the present. I trust the future handsomely, as you already know, but my own concerns have been with my own few centuries. When I die—probably in a year, or it may be two—I shall be laid beside my wife; and having planted hawthorns over me, the duty of the community, so far as I am concerned, will be at an end. The greater duty to themselves I do not seek to influence. Some will probably desire to remain; others, to return to the larger world and the complexities of a higher civilisation than ours. Probsire to remain; others, to return to the larger world and ably Dragonsville will disappear, when the walls return to the earth from which they were raised; and if a measure of what I have endeavoured to do and advance is carried into the greater world and proves, in its small way, of any service, I shall not have lived in vain."

Sir Jasper nodded.

"I am deeply impressed and much edified," he declared; "but I do not think you must ask me to stop with you. To break a precedent is a pity, and the life frankly invites me by reason of its simplicity, dignity and general charm; but my aim and purpose have ever been to redress wrong and fight evil. Here things are so happily ordered that an armed knight—a man of war such as myself—whose business is to destroy the enemies of mankind and strike bitter and bloody blows that the world may be cleaner, safer and happier—such a man, honourable Dragon, would find nothing to do in this place."

"Why not beat your sword into a ploughshare, your lance into a pruning hook, your armour into kitchen utensils?" asked the other. "I can imagine your silver helmet making an exquisite holder for a pot plant in the boudoir of my dear Lilian."

A slight warmth of colour mantled the cheek of the hero.

"You are not quite as ingenuous as you pretend, I fear," he answered.

"Consult her," urged the Lavender Dragon. "You might do worse, for to her outward charm is united a very beautiful mind, and I have little doubt that, in reality, she comes of descent as long and noble as your own. Take occasion to have discourse with her before you decide. Speaking generally, your argument is capable of refutation, for the gift of skill in the field is not, I think, your sole claim to distinction. Given good will, the prime motive power of all progress, and a desire to help our body politic, a man of your high principles and exalted sentiments should not be at a loss even here. I, for example, shall beg you to throw light upon much that puzzles my dragon mind. To-day I have done all the talking, but think not that I cannot listen too. Many of my friends and neighbours have helped me vastly with their practical knowledge of your species, and the rising generation is not backward of still more valuable ideas. However, you are free to go when you please; but I should think it courteous and considerate if you would undertake to stay a month with us."

"That I will gladly do," replied his guest. "There is, however, one privilege I would beg. My squire, George Pipkin, must be suffering the extremity of grief on my account, and he will, not unnaturally, fear for me a very different fate than this I now enjoy. Is it within your power, think you, to unite us? I may tell you that he will certainly seek me and push his way, sooner or later, to your outer walls. If, on reaching them, he might be admitted into this happy land, I should thank you heartily."

"I will bring him myself," promised the Lavender Dragon. "A man so faithful and of such devotion to his master is worthy of all respect."

Sir Jasper sighed and reviewed his tremendous experience.

"What the world would think of me, I cannot guess," he said.

"What the world thinks of us is of prodigious unimportance, my friend," replied the saurian. "The only thing that really matters is what we think of ourselves. In nothing is reason so flouted as in our ridiculous self-estimates; but when we suffer her to help us read our own hearts and judge the real worth of our own abilities and ambitions, then we shall begin to know what moral progress may mean."

VII

GREAT NEWS FOR GEORGE PIPKIN

EARLY ON the morrow the Lavender Dragon set forth to seek George Pipkin and, after sleeping soundly in a most comfortable and cheerful chamber, the latest arrival at Dragonsville went among the people and saw and heard much that gave him pleasure.

His host had not returned at the hour of midday dinner, but certain elderly and dignified persons of both sexes joined Sir Jasper at the meal. He found Father Lazarus, the priest, to be of the party, together with Nicholas Warrender, the seneschal, a grey-haired dame or two, and an old but venerable man whom the others addressed as "Sir Claude." There were also present Amory Doncaster, the Lavender

Dragon's doctor, and Lilian Lovenot, who, radiant in a gown of azure blue, decorated with pearls as large as filberts, sat beside the new-comer.

Conversation proved by no means parochial and his new friends manifested great interest in Sir Jasper's professional experiences and the doings of the outer world. The old people expressed a hope that life ran in more gracious channels than of yore, and that he found an increase of prosperity and happiness upon his travels; while, when he confessed that new wars were in the making and new discontents battering and bruising humanity on every side, the younger men and women present declared their impatience and indignation at the slow progress of the race.

"I cannot but think," said Lilian Lovenot, "that a time is near when the rising generation of Dragonsville will be called to abandon this life of ease and happiness, and go forth to carry the principles and theories of L.D. into the outer darkness."

"A tremendous opinion," replied a youth by the name of Howard Harris. "But it may come to that. We have all made one another as happy as it is possible to be at Dragonsville, and, for my own part, I sometimes sigh for other fields wherein to conquer."

"Or be conquered," said Sir Claude, and looking upon Mm, the younger knight observed the first face in this city which betokened a mind not wholly at rest.

After the meal was ended, Sir Jasper, his fellow knight and Lilian walked to the grave of the Lavender Dragon's wife and sat upon it under the shadow of the flowering shrubs. Then Sir Claude, having found that his own adventures in chivalry belonged to a period far anterior to the visitor's, explained the reason of that settled melancholy which appeared upon his grey and wrinkled countenance.

"I am Sir Claude Pontifex Fortescue, of the Strong Shield," he said, "and it was I, Sir Jasper, who, sixty years ago, laid lance in rest against L.D. That awful error of judgment has haunted me and cast the sour shadow of remorse upon my long, and, I hope, subsequently blameless career."

"I did no less in thought," confessed Sir Jasper. "My one desire was to slaughter this prodigious person and cut his head off. Surely he is the last to blame you, or harbour any suspicion of resentment. It is summed in a word, Sir Knight; you and I knew no better. I will go further and declare that there was no reason why we should."

"Exactly; and he has told you so a dozen times, Sir Claude," added Lilian. "It is irrational of you to harbour this sorrow for more than half a century. You merely scratched his side and did not shorten his precious life by an hour."

The ancient knight only shook his head.

"I deserved death, for he strove to address me before I charged, and I would not listen."

"But he spared you to be useful; and no doubt you have been useful," suggested Sir Jasper.

"He has," vowed Lilian. "L.D. himself declares that Sir Claude has been his right paw for sixty years."

But Sir Claude dwelt morbidly on the details of that far-away disaster.

"He merely thumped me; then he brought me here, healed my bruises and exalted me into a position of trust and honour. Would that I had been worthy of such forgiveness, my friends."

He refused to be comforted, and presently Sir Jasper and Lilian left him, still sighing to himself, and went their way through the gardens of the castle.

"Come and look at our carpet bedding," suggested the beautiful maiden, and her companion soon stood where five-and-twenty gardeners were busy arranging a little horticultural surprise for the dragon on his return. Sir Jasper, however, was no authority on these subjects and he turned the conversation into more personal channels. Lilian, at his entreaty, related the brief particulars of her own career as far as she remembered it; but she shared the dragon's opinion concerning her advent into the world and agreed with the inhabitants of Pongley-in-the-Marsh that the excellent Lovenots were not her parents.

"I loved them dearly," she said, "but I never felt towards them as a daughter, and when L.D. discovered me weeping at the well, he knew, by a marvellous intuition peculiar to him and doubtless the result of his vast experience, that I was no true child of the hamlet."

"Here you are happier?" inquired the knight.

"It may sound ungrateful, but I am. I do love comfort and cleanliness and, I am afraid, luxury," confessed Lilian. "Silk next the skin, swansdown to sleep upon, crystal to drink out of, instead of cloam, and so on—weak—very weak, Sir Jasper."

"Doubtless the blood in your veins demands these modest additions to life," he declared. "There can be no sort of doubt that the fairies, after their somewhat malicious custom, played a trick upon your foster-mother and your real one; and now the daughter of the Lovenots probably occupies a position of high estate and has usurped your connections and your lawful style and title."

"It may be so, but I am perfectly happy here," said Lilian. "In the fragrant atmosphere of the Lavender Dragon, we live a life of such fine quality that no distinction could better it. I naturally mourn my own dear parents sometimes, and wonder what they make of the girl who bears my name, whatever that may be; but I daresay they have found a better daughter than I should have been to them."

"That is quite impossible," he asserted, and was lost in thought for the space of twenty minutes.

Sir Jasper then spoke again and put a question.

"Is it beyond reason that I should be permitted to gaze at your left elbow?" he inquired, and the lady started at a request so unusual.

"Who told you about that, Sir Jasper?" she asked in her turn.

"Nobody told me anything, fair mistress; but, as they say, the world is small, and I have in my mind a noble West-country family, who lost a daughter and found a changeling under somewhat distressing circumstances about sixteen years ago. The changeling ran away with a wine-drawer when she was fifteen, and no great search was made to find either of them. The noble family of the Traceys, who are always said to have the wind in their faces, happen to be

neighbours of my own kin, and we are therefore familiar with a tradition among them. The eldest son always exhibits a birthmark on
his left shoulder-blade in the shape of a poignard; while the eldest
daughter's left elbow never fails to reveal an auburn mole in shape
of a cuddy wren."

Lilian's aquamarine eyes shone like ocean pools when the tide is
out, and she exhibited the wildest astonishment.

"But I have a little wren upon my left elbow," she cried.

"Then you are the vanished daughter of the far-famed Lord
Meavybrook, of the family of Tracey in the West country, whose
manor adjoins our lands of Pomeroy. I salute Mistress Lovenot no
longer, but the Honourable Camilla Petronell Thomasin Tracey and
kiss her hand!"

At this dramatic moment a shadow fell upon the carpet bedding,
and the aerial music of the Lavender Dragon's wings announced his
return. In a few moments he had descended, whereupon George
Pipkin and his roan charger reached the ground together. Instantly
George perceived his master and, rushing to him, praised God and
flung himself at Sir Jasper's feet. The knight raised his squire, cheered
him heartily, bade him rejoice, assured him that all was well, and
presently surrendered him to the good offices of half a dozen friendly
spirits, who hastened to pleasure the new arrival.

The translated maiden meantime attended upon the dragon, and,
after L.D. had enjoyed a mighty meal of hay and fine oats, informed
him of the amazing discovery concerning herself. He was gratified
but by no means surprised, and when Sir Jasper returned from a talk
with George, all particulars were demanded.

The knight, however, could add no more to the story than he had
already told. He was permitted to study the white elbow of the lady
and there, exquisitely fashioned by Nature's self, appeared a wee
cuddy wren that, upon the milky purity of the skin, suggested an
agate cameo carved by a master's hand.

"One takes these happenings in a large spirit," said the dragon.
"I am well-pleased to have my intuition proved correct, and for the

moment only a single thought occurs to me. We have now a choice of three names for Mistress Tracey, and what I want to know is this: does she desire that we call her henceforth Camilla, Petronell, or Thomasin?"

The girl looked at Sir Jasper and smiled so radiantly that a mavis on a bough burst into music and added certain notes to his repertory that have been in every grey bird's song since then.

"It is Sir Jasper, after my gossips, who has given me these pleasant names," she said; "he shall, therefore, determine by which I must henceforth be addressed."

"Let L.D. choose," begged the knight, but the dragon declined.

"Then let it be Camilla on Sundays and Petronell through the week, save upon Fridays, when she shall be called Thomasin."

It was decided so, and in high good humour the Lavender Dragon retired to sleep, and the knight and the lady were again left in each other's company.

Strange emotions already agitated Sir Jasper and he found in his mind a new sensation, which left him a little bemused. Bitter-sweet under-currents of. thought possessed him and led to some slight loss of manners; for so occupied was he with his own reflections that more than once he forgot to reply when Petronell questioned him, and thrice he permitted himself to gaze upon her with a direct glare of his blue eyes that cast her into maidenly confusion.

For these lapses he apologised in stumbling words, and he had no sooner done so when he committed the like errors again. Anon she left him and walked pensively to the castle, while he returned to George. Pipkin was now well fed and had changed his travel-stained jerkin of leather and oft-mended boots for a murry-coloured velvet tunic and small clothes of orange-tawny laced with black. He had entirely recovered from the shock of the morning, and having related how the dragon had snapped him, as he was about to plunge into the Woods of Blore, he dismissed the subject and declared his great satisfaction at the turn of events.

"I have never had such a fuss made about me since I was short-coated," declared the squire, "and I am well content to enjoy a long respite and rest from our tedious life among these delightful people. May I venture to hope, Sir Jasper, that you design to remain here at least until the autumn?"

But his master thought differently.

"This is no place for us, George," he replied. "A month I have undertaken to remain, that I may study a society from which we can both learn much to our profit; but that done, we take the road. We are men of war, and there is nothing that we can accomplish to add to the perfection of this peaceful community. We will, therefore, glean what wisdom we may and, fortified thereby, return to our own good work."

Pipkin, however, secretly hoped their visit might be prolonged; and then a curious accident brought the squire face to face with one whom he had known in the outer world.

They were strolling down a little street together, wherein every house seemed to smile an invitation upon them from its open door and cheerful countenance, when, out of a cot, in whose garden towered purple columbines above a bed of rosemary, there tripped a young woman and two children. She was dark and comely, with black hair, brown eyes and a skin as ruddy as a burn in spate. The youngsters were like her—a pair of bright-eyed boys with laughing eyes.

"Odds bodikins!" cried George. "Here is Sally Slater, the widow of West Fell. What chance has brought her to this happy valley?"

The woman's eyes now fell on George and she recognised him.

"'Tis Master Pipkin!" she cried.

"By our Lady I command you tell me how you came hither," demanded George, and Sally Slater related her strange story.

"You must know that after my husband died, I took care of his old mother, and on a day when I made for her a brew of lentils, herbs and milk, an awful fate befell me. I was engaged in my cooking and thinking with tears of my departed spouse, when into my cabin burst half a dozen strange men. There was a witch hunt through West Fell, and seeing me about my pot, the cruel wretches leapt upon me and haled me before a judge. As ill fortune would have it, a black cat with green eyes purred upon my hearth at the time, while in a corner, for I was ever a cleanly woman, there stood a great birch broom. Here was sufficient evidence to endanger my existence, and after I had sworn, by the blood of our Saviour, that I was no witch and had never in all my life held commune with the Fiend, they put me to the torture to make me confess.

"They thrust me into a chair of sharp steel spikes; they dropped boiling oil upon my legs and bosom and held a lighted taper under my armpits. And then, after striving with my poor might to hold to the truth, my body's grief was too great and, even for the brief respite, which I knew was all that remained, I lied and screamed out that I was indeed a witch."

Sir Jasper regarded poor Sally with sorrow.

"It is even so with thousands," he said. "For the brief surcease of their agony, tormented flesh cries out a falsehood, and so men and women without number are forced to say what is false and condemn themselves to death; while those who think they do God service, rejoice and cast the unfortunate innocents into the fire. The Popes of Rome swept away that legal justice enjoyed by all accused persons under pagan law, and our most earnest Christians have sent innumerable harmless men and women to the flames on this account. Fear was responsible for these cruelties, and fear makes all men unjust. Fear surely must it have been that caused Elisha to consign the children to the bears, though why he was alarmed at two score noisy youngsters, we shall never know. And the men who have accomplished these dismal feats were the salt of the earth! The good Bishop of Treves burned six thousand, five hundred parishioners and desolated his diocese; Nicholas Remy, a pious and, I believe, a pleasing person in his home, roasted over eight hundred of his poor and powerless fellow creatures. One remembers also that admirable Protestant jurist, Benedict Carpzor, who not only read the Holy Bible from cover to cover fifty-three times, but also passed twenty thousand sentences of death on witches and sorcerers."

"Did no ghosts ever haunt or distract these accursed wretches?" cried George Pipkin.

"Certainly not," replied the knight. "They passed to their eternal reward with the blessing and applause of all men, and in conscious-ness of lives nobly spent on their Maker's business. In the case of Remy aforesaid, however, it is reported that he was unhappy on his deathbed because, in a moment of human weakness, he had only scourged certain young children naked round the pyres whereon their parents were burning, instead of casting them into the flames also. His conscience pricked him sharply in that matter at the end, for it is well known, and Mother Church is clear upon the subject, that the children of witches have the Devil for their sire and should never be spared the stake."

"Then how come you and your brave boys to be alive, Sally?" inquired George.

"Thanks entirely to L.D.," replied the young widow. "By the will of God, he was passing West Fell when I went to the faggots, and scarcely had they been ignited before he came to earth, sent the peo-ple flying in every direction and bore me away. Nor did his mercy end with my rescue. As soon as we had landed here and I learned the truth of him, my mother's heart cried for my children. I explained that they would certainly be burned alive after our departure, and were probably already beyond salvation. Whereon he instantly set out again, and West Fell, being cast into a great terror by his visit, the children were still in the land of the living. Certain persons had pitied them in secret and bidden them fly before it was too late. Our dragon came upon the little things lying asleep together without the village, and when they awakened from their journey, it was in my arms."

"All's well that ends well," said George, "and now tell me a little about our native place. I often think of West Fell and my family."

Sally showed some uneasiness.

"I'm very much afraid there will be bad news for you, Master Pip-kin, when you gang home again," she said.

"Let me have it," he answered, "for as to ganging home, I do not feel in any violent haste to be there."

"Poor Mistress Pipkin is gathered in," said Sally sadly. "A year or so before my troubles, she went to pick water-cresses in the owl-light, and 'tis feared she mistook the way. Be that as it will, they found her drowned with a very peaceful expression upon her face."

"My stars, Jemima gone!" cried George, staring before him with more astonishment than grief. "Are you sure of what you are telling me, Sally?"

"She lies beside the little one took after he was born; and your daughter has married the cordwainer, John Bindle, and your son has gone for a sailor in one of the king's ships."

"This would seem to be the day of my life!" murmured Pipkin.

"Accept hearty sympathy in your affliction," said Sir Jasper. "You will suffer this blow with your usual philosophic fortitude, George."

"Heaven helping, I shall make shift to face it," answered the widower, "for what saith the Book? 'He hath done all things well.' "

VIII

THREE SONGS AND A STORY

THIS BEING no tale of love, we are not so much concerned with the swift and ingenuous romance of Sir Jasper and his honourable lady, as challenged by the result of their common passion. Nor can we dwell overmuch upon the less emotional love-making of George Pipkin, who, before he had resided a week at Dragonsville, was resolutely courting Sally Slater and winning the affection of her sons.

Sir Jasper now found himself at odds between love and duty, yet opposed the one against the other with diminishing zest, for as time passed, he could not fail to observe that the maiden of his adoration was by no means impatient of his company. The knight's cheek grew lean, and his blue eyes became anxious. He had little intelligence, but a conscience of almost morbid activity, and at first he suspected the whole business to be enchantment—a possible wile of the Lavender Dragon to detain him indefinitely, fog his senses and deaden his soul to the clarion of duty. But though enchanting, there was nothing in the attitude of Petronell to suggest that she played a part, endeavoured to enchain Sir Jasper, or come between him and his appointed task. Indeed she delighted to hear of his modest achievements and gave it as her opinion that his career had only just begun. His aspirations were her own, for now she openly longed to be of use in the world and carry the lessons learned at Dragonsville to Devonshire at some future time.

"To do good is an art," she declared, "and needs as much practising as any other. It is, indeed, because the beginner often makes such a mess of it that many are choked off well-doing altogether and turn to other and easier pursuits.

"It is understood," she continued, "that so long as L.D. shall live, I do not leave him; and much I wish, dear knight, you found it possible to make the same promise. To think of the world without him, is to think of a very sad thing; but he is rarely mistaken, and in his opinion he will pass during the spring of next year. Then such as desire to stay and proceed with their lives after his fashion, will do so; but not a few of the rising generation propose to explore the world. Whether their discoveries will turn their feet hither again, who can say? For my part, I was in a mind to stop among those I love and cherish here; but after your astounding information, it is clearly my duty to go home, reveal my birth-mark and claim my parentage."

"I agree with you, Camilla," declared Sir Jasper, for it was a Sunday on which these words were spoken, and the knight and the lady returned, side by side, to the Castle from Morning Prayer.

"It is our Lavender Dragon's own wish that I should do so," she continued. "Indeed, since he has learned the truth about me, he has even raised the question whether I do well to tarry at all. But my father and mother have waited so many years that it cannot harm them to bide still longer in ignorance; and I will never leave L.D. while he lives. I owe him the little wisdom I possess, and I shall strive to plan my future life by his precepts wherever I may spend it."

A vision of amazing beauty stole into the thoughts of Sir Jasper. He pictured himself returning to the West country with a bride; he saw the great houses of Tracey and Pomeroy gloriously united; he pictured the joy of all concerned, the rejoicings, the largesse flying in silver showers, even the red Devon ox, roasted whole, and the morris dances, cudgel play, bull baiting and other delights of Merrie England proper to such an occasion. Incidentally he saw a ring fence round the two manors.

But he kept these dreams to himself. He had reached a stage at which the next step must be a declaration of marriage, or speedy departure, and he suspected that the lady was of the same opinion. But still he hesitated, until it wanted but three days before the month was ended and his undertaking to remain at Dragonsville absolved. He felt in dire need of another opinion at this juncture, for spiritual uneasiness overtook him in the night watches and he doubted whether these earthly ambitions much became him. To consult George Pipkin was idle. The squire had already become affianced to Sally Slater, and the folk congratulated both man and woman, for George, a resourceful person and quick to respond to friendship, became a favourite from the first. He knew Sir Jasper's plight very well indeed, for his master could not conceal it. In truth, everybody was alive to the situation and when, finally, the lovesick fellow determined to lay the matter before L.D. himself, his host showed no surprise. They spoke together after knight and dragon had bathed side by side in the great central fountain, before breakfast on a cloudless morning of July; and while the rising sun glittered over the rose and azure scales of the larger animal and quickly dried them, Sir Jasper, having resumed his garments, explained the problem and humbly invited comments and a solution.

"I, of course, am an 'intellectual' and apologise for it," answered L.D. "It is comparatively easy to write, or lecture, eat hay, drink water and tell everybody else what they ought to do. This rule of life gives those who practise it enormous satisfaction and induces them to suppose that they are the only people who really much matter to the cosmic scheme. But as I find that to devour red meat, drink red wine and do things, instead of telling other people to do them, is much more difficult, my admiration has always been reserved for such as themselves attempt to advance the work of the world. To pull down is easier than to build up, and I am entirely on the side of those who would build, even if their building be faulty; while they who snap and snarl and spew opposition on everybody who is honestly seeking to help distracted humanity, leave me cold—even for the cold-blooded reptile which I happen to be. In a word, it may be said that the heart of man seeks to build, while the brain of him is chiefly concerned to destroy the existing order. Both are right and both are vital; and when they work together in the light of reason, good things must happen. But when will they?

"Now, you are of the thick-headed, but warm-hearted, order of men who want to get on with it. And you have fallen in love with a maiden suited to you in every possible way. She belongs to your own order, though that matters nothing; but what does matter is that she also belongs to your own sort of intelligence. She prays to the same God, as far as it can be said that any two people have the same idea of what their Maker means; she enjoys the same humanist outlook; she resents the same wrongs and evils; she is quite as determined as yourself to leave the world better than she finds it. What more seemly and fitting, then, than that you twain should wed and presently go forth, nerved and heartened each by the other, in the glory of a shared love, a shared trust, and a shared duty to the world? She has already made you happier than she found you, though at present you do not look it; and you have brought into her delightful life a deep and mysterious quickening and wakened her noblest emotions. Thus you have both made the world happier than you found it already, and what is worrying you is a chimera, a vague and futile echo of that melancholy hoot, a vanished order of Christians raised from their burrows, caves and catacombs. The idea of these estimable, but mistaken, cenobites, you will recollect. They held no happiness seemly in this life, and accounted human love the invention of the Devil. They did their best to depopulate the earth; but their claim and clamour were alike unavailing in the face of Nature, and to-day we all, I think, admit that it is a very seemly and blessed thing for a healthy man to marry the right woman and to take a hand in the next generation. But that is a subject not likely to interest you for the moment. Therefore place your heart at Petronell's feet, and if she prove willing to pick it up, wed her, stay with me, as she intends to do, until I go underground—somewhere about the breaking of the leaf next year—and then seek your relations together, and go on doing your duty to the best of your united powers."

"You have greatly heartened me, my noble friend," answered Sir Jasper. "It is almost beyond the dreams of ambition that such a maiden can stoop to such a man; but I will at least summon courage to approach her; and if the answer doom me to everlasting sorrow, you will not take it amiss that I mount my steed, don my armour and go hence."

"Certainly not," replied the devious dragon, who already knew that Petronell loved the lad with devotion. "If she say you nay, I shall be the first to speed the parting guest."

Within a week, however, the young people were betrothed, much to their own delight and the satisfaction of the entire community. The Lavender Dragon, who never lost an occasion to bring his friends together, proclaimed a banquet and entertainment of unexampled splendour to celebrate this engagement, and it was swiftly planned that both Sir Jasper and his squire should be wedded in the same hour, upon a day after the harvest had been reaped.

Nicholas Warrender, the dragon's old seneschal, was master of the ceremonies on the occasion of this public entertainment; all Dragonsville came to L.D.'s revel, and features of the joyful event were certain performances which followed a great midday meal. There was dancing; there was singing; there were athletic sports and trials of strength and dexterity. But the special attraction, and that most vividly remembered, remained to the credit of Sir Jasper and his bride, George Pipkin, and the Lavender Dragon himself.

The knight, his lady and his squire each obliged with a song; while L.D. told the people a new story.

Sir Jasper's betrothed sang first, and accompanied herself upon a lute. The lyric had been composed for that instrument, and Petronell sang with great charm and natural feeling, though, as she confessed, there was nothing to admire in either the words, or the music. Yet it happened that this was the only song she knew: her foster-mother had taught it to her in childhood.

Song for a Lute

"Margery, Merle and Aveline—
And rarest, fairest Aveline,
Loveliest maids that ever were seen—
Loveliest ever seen,
Wandered beneath the hunter's moon—
The red, uprising hunter's moon,
For to find the fairies and beg a boon —
    Ting-a-ling! Ting-a-ling!
    Ting! Ting! Ting-a-ling!
Beg for a pixy boon.

"There came a boy along the way—
A pretty boy along the way,
And Margery stopped with him to play—
Margery stopped to play.
Her sisters went through dimpsy light,
By dingles dim through dimpsy light,
And tears of one were falling bright —
    Ting-a-ling! Ting-a-ling!
    Ting! Ting! Ting-a-ling!
Tears, they were falling bright.

"A convent by the way they trod—
  The dark and dusky path they trod,
  Drew weeping Merle at the will of God—
  Merle by the will of God.
  She entered, and she bides there yet—
  A sainted nun she bides there yet,
  For love of the boy that Margery met —
      Ting-a-ling! Ting-a-ling!
        Ting! Ting! Ting-a-ling!
  Boy that Margery met.

"But Aveline by beck and glen—
  By starry beck and moony glen
  Won to the holt of the pixy men—
  Haunt of the pixy men.
  And thus spake they to Aveline—
  To rarest, fairest Aveline,
'When the King sees you, he'll forget the Queen!'
  Ting-a-ling! Ting-a-ling!
        Ting! Ting! Ting-a-ling-a-ling-a-ling!
  King shall forget the Queen!'"

Everybody applauded Petronell's singing and refrained from crit-
icising the song; but Sir Jasper held the accompaniment to be very
beautiful, and the dragon, who used an ear-trumpet on special occasions, declared the melody tuneful, and hoped that the lady would
sing it many times to him, so that he might better appreciate it; for of
music he knew nothing.

Then Sir Jasper, having indicated to Petronell the tune which she
must play upon her lute to accompany his song, made ready.

"I will give you 'The Charm,' " he said, "and, though it is long
since I had occasion to sing and I am much out of practice, I will
do my best."

He proceeded in a not unmusical baritone.

The Charm

"When chafers drone their litany
And pray, Oh, 'Father, grant that we
From airy-mouse delivered be,'
Go seek—go seek the Charm.

"Under the sky, when a star shoots,
Beneath an oak, when owlet hoots,
Gather ye simples, dig ye roots
To build—to build the Charm.

"That glassy ghost upon a thorn—
The raiment of a snake outworn—
Bust backward though the dark be borne
To feed—to feed the Charm.

"A glow-worm—she whose gentle light
Glimmers green-gold upon the night,
Beside yon churchyard aconite—
Shall help—shall help the Charm.

"One willow from the cradle take,
Where a boy baby lies awake,
And splinters off a coffin break
To fortify the Charm.

"A tarnished silver chalice bring
Dead gossips gave at christening,
And dip the moonlight from a spring
To crown—to crown the Charm.

"This much, God wot, a child might do,
Yet all must fail if haply you

Lack a child's faith, so trusting, true
To bless—to bless the Charm.

"Many the spells of high degree
And fruitful happiness, we see
All lost for faith to set them free
And work—and work the Charm."

"An excellent song with an excellent moral," declared Nicholas Warrender. "But rather monotonous."

"That is my fault," confessed Sir Jasper. "If I had sung it better, I think that you would have liked it better."

"Or if I had played it better," added the musician.

Then spoke Sally Slater, who was going to marry Master Pipkin.

"If you please, dear L.D., I don't think you will like George's song, and it may be better if he is silent."

"Why, Sally?" asked the dragon kindly. "I do not think that George would sing anything unfit for our ears."

"That's just what he's going to do," declared Sally, whose face was red and whose eyes were anxious.

"Explain before you proceed, George," suggested Sir Jasper.

"It's like this," said the squire. "I'm not wishful to sing if none is wishful to hear. To be honest, the song is about a louse—and why not?"

"There's not a louse in Dragonsville," declared the seneschal with conviction.

"Nevertheless, there are many elsewhere," replied George, "and God made them for His own dark purposes."

The dragon spoke.

"Numerous creatures are quite familiar to us," he said, "and not a few seek the hospitality of our homes and persons, whether we cold-shoulder them or no. They have their own methods of circumventing our hostility, and the black-beetle persists from generation to generation; the rat survives, with a determined resistance, despite all that we do against him; the wolf still makes shift to rear his family and trouble our shepherds; while many lesser things cling closer than a brother and will not be denied. Let us by all means pursue our warfare against them; but let us be just to our enemies, and if some human poet has struck his lyre to the body-louse, that is his affair. I see no objection to hearing what he has to say upon the subject with an open mind."

Thus encouraged, George stood forth; but Petronell did not offer to accompany him.

"The song is in two parts, if you please," explained Pipkin. "The first part is the louse talking to his Maker."

He then sang these words in a deep and sonorous bass, which the dragon had no difficulty in hearing.

A Chat

Pediculus
"Almighty One, I grieve to find
   That in your everlasting nous
   For reasons hidden from my mind,
   Your servant you have made a louse.

"It was your parasitic whim
   All creatures that on earth do dwell,
   Whether they walk, or fly, or swim,
   Should each one give some brother hell.

"From royal lion to agile flea,
   Your all-embracing scheme was laid;
   From genus homo down to me
   The case is thus, I am afraid.

"But man's the super-louse of earth;
   He crawls its face, deflowers, defames,
   Devours, destroys, brings rapine, dearth,
   Deliriums and deaths and shames.

"So what were meaner, viler, worse
Than my hard fate—a louse of lice!
Oh, Father of the Universe,
It isn't nice; it isn't nice!"

The singer here broke off and addressed the Lavender Dragon. He felt conscious that the audience was against him.

"That's what the creature said to the Creator, your honour; and now, whether they like it or no, I'm going to sing what he got for his answer."

"Certainly, George; one side is only good till we hear the other," answered L.D. courteously, and Pipkin finished thus:

Omnipotence
"My humble friend, take heart of grace;
There's many a miracle of Mine
Compared with which your homely race
May honestly be said to shine.

"You are a polished gem beside
The micrococcus I have made;
Your shapely stature, easy stride
Put bacillus quite in the shade.

"But they, and you, and such small fry
Of matter fashioned to assail
Humanity, stand fairly high
In your Creator's social scale.

"My master-piece and prime device—
My highest flight and true top-hole
Of loathsome horror—are the lice
I send to bite the human soul.

"Could them you see your heart would freeze
Such loathly spectacles to view.

Be of good cheer: compared with these,
A little gentleman are you!"

There was an ominous silence and nobody applauded.

"I told you they'd hate it," said Sally.

"A painful theme, George," declared the dragon. "Nevertheless I am glad to have heard the song. There is truth in it; but like so many other true things—— You might write the words from George's dictation, Petronell, then I will consider them in private. Do not, however, sing it again. Sally will teach you some sunnier ditties. Your voice is admirable."

After further conversation upon this subject, during which George found the sense of the company against him and learned, to his confusion, from Father Lazarus, that his performance approached, if it did not actually attain, blasphemy, the seneschal called for silence and the dragon made a few remarks before telling his story.

"As you know," he said, "all my stories have a moral, and the story that dares to convey a moral must be extra good, or young people naturally scorn it and grown-up people decline to hear it. A time is fast coming when no story will be permitted any moral whatever, and those who attempt stories with morals will be derided for their pains; but I belong to the old guard in this matter, and the adventure of a mighty monarch I am now about to relate cannot be denied its conclusions. Understand, however, that I do not draw them. I leave them entirely to the listener, who shall apply or ignore them as he may prefer."

The dragon then told his tale, slowly and solemnly. He was himself so impressed by its moral implications, that he quite failed to see the funny side, or if he did see it, he pretended not to do so.

Sesostris

This was the name given by the Greeks to that very distinguished King of Egypt, more generally known as Rameses II, and I shall tell you a pleasing incident in his career, which reveals this great man to have possessed an element of common sense rarely met with among early potentates, who possessed supreme power and held life and death in their hands. Sesostris enjoyed a plenitude of might and glory sufficient to turn the head of any lesser king, nor did he deny himself a certain amount of barbaric licence, or decline to accept what passed for pleasure in those remote times.

For example, consider the chariot that he used upon great occasions of State, and, what is still more wonderful to tell, the animals that drew it. The vehicle itself was constructed of gold and ivory and composed entirely of the fruits won from victorious invasions. It had been encrusted with magnificent gems—ruby, sapphire, and diamond—and cunningly wrought to flash its splendor even on a dull day. Sesostris himself drove his coach and four and he never failed to attract a multitude of shouting admirers, for not horse or ass, zebu or zebra, ostrich or cameleopard drew him. Four captive kings strained at the harness; and though Sesostris swung and cracked a formidable whip behind these fallen rulers, in justice to a great man we record that he never touched his team with it. Such an equipage was not contrived for speed, but arrogant pomp alone.

Never the stars in all their courses had witnessed any such tremendous sight as these royal slaves dragging Sesostris about the streets of Thebes, or Luxor. Tyrants were they, made prisoners in war, and even their own old subjects would sometimes travel to see this astounding turn-out, and tremble to witness their monarchs transformed into beasts of burden.

Of these four rulers condemned to this appalling penalty for unsuccess, one was a Syrian of ripe age. He occupied the near off position, and upon an occasion when Sesostris proceeded to offer sacrifice for a good Nile at the temple of Apis, the royal driver observed this chieftain cast repeated back glances of extraordinary interest and awe at the golden wheel of the chariot immediately behind him.

"O King," enquired Sesostris, pulling up, "do you find anything amiss?"

"Not so, Glory of the Earth, and Life of your People," answered the Syrian humbly.

"Then what are you staring at?" asked the ruler of Egypt.

"Sire," replied the elder. "It happens that we may live a great part of our lives with some familiar, necessary object and then, suddenly, at chance prompting of the intellect, or flash of intuition, perceive in the everyday thing a fresh meaning, an added significance, that lifts our homely invention to new and notable seriousness, if not solemnity."

"There is nothing in the least solemn about a chariot wheel, though, seeing that the spokes were fashioned out of the tusks of your late herd of white elephants, they doubtless turn your thoughts to gravity," replied Sesostris.

"They do indeed," confessed his royal slave. "But it is the opera-tion rather than construction of these ivory spokes that gives me my great thought. Herein I find a parable of enormous significance, and only wonder how the mightiest brain on the earth at this moment has failed to note it."

"You refer to me, no doubt," replied Sesostris, "and you may rest assured that I have not missed the meaning of the wheel in our affairs. Surely the wheel of the potter and the wheel of the vehicle are landmarks in all human history."

"There is even more than that I have discerned," answered the Syrian, "for behold, as the wheel turns round, how the spoke now nighest earth slowly ascends until it is above all the other spokes and pointing heavenwards; but even in the moment of its highest ascension, steadily and certainly, as the wheel comes full circle, it sinks and sinks, until it is upon the earth again, while another has taken its pride of place aloft. O, Glory of the Universe and Topmost Spoke in the Wheel of the Children of Men, does not this formidable spectacle appal your heart and chill the purple blood in your most honourable veins?"

Doubtless a lesser man might have resented such a sermon at such a time and commanded the preacher to lay hold and get on with his task; but Sesostris, if his mind was not of that majestic dimension his oriental flatterer pretended, had none the less a very keen wit, and the parable was well calculated to challenge his practical wisdom and sense of reality. For a moment he remained silent, weighing the measure of the thing spoken; and then, with a certain impulsive and honest habit of mind peculiar to him, he spoke.

"Hear us, my people, and you, our steeds, also give ear. The thing that this learned tyrant of the East has imparted to us, we find to be rich with great meaning; and since the grass is never allowed to grow beneath our royal feet, we determine from this moment to change our mode of traction, and travel henceforth in a manner more fitted to human reason and kingly decorum. Greater is that monarch who walks afoot than he who subjects any fellow man to the indignity of the shafts."

Amazed, all listened, and then Sesostris turned to his captives and spoke with a swift and regal generosity.

"Kings," said he, "we had permitted ourselves to overlook the way of fate and the immutable vicissitude of every human lot. This grey-haired Syrian is exceedingly right, even though he has proved us to be exceedingly wrong. Depart in peace, free men—all four of you! Return to your nations, that you may govern them with justice and mercy; and take along with you from our treasure houses, wondrous gifts for each wife and child, together with rations for your journeys and an escort worthy of the occasion and its demands. And never more, in this, our little and uncertain life, let warfare and hatred arise between us to mar our future friendship."

He descended from his chariot, embraced each bewildered monarch and kissed the aged Syrian on both cheeks. Then, raising his hand to stay the shout of applause lifted around him by the younger generation of his people, for his counsellors were rather quiet, he spoke again.

"Henceforward, Egypt, when our chariot passes in affairs demanding circumstance and glory, it shall be drawn by two grey donkeys, in token of that common sense which is at the root of all progress honestly to be described as royal. And may they never find any need to talk to us!"

This ended the story of the Lavender Dragon, and the company streamed out over the Castle grounds, to enjoy dancing, archery, quarterstaff and other diversions. L.D. himself presented the prizes—a bunch of flowers for each maiden, a wreath of oak leaves for the men.

IX

ANOTHER DRAGON GIVES A LOUDER ROAR

THE EVENT of the autumn at Dragonsville was the erection of two dwellings, one for Sir Jasper and his bride, the other for George Pipkin, Sally Slater and her sons. According to the custom of the country, Sir Jasper was allowed no hand in his own habitation; but he worked as diligently as the rest to make his squire's future home both dignified and comfortable. Petronell, too, lent her aid, and when the walls were raised she painted beautiful pictures inside them; while upon a knoll hard by, overlooking the river, George Pipkin and half a hundred willing workers erected a considerable villa for the knight and his lady.

The weddings were arranged for an early date in October; but while yet the sun held strength to make the autumn foliage gay and gild the ripening berries on briar and thorn, there came a remarkable visitor to Dragonsville.

At dawn on a cloudy autumn morning, a strange dragon was seen bathing his mighty limbs in the great central fountain, and while the creature appeared to be smaller than L.D., none could fail to observe a certain family resemblance. The veteran of Dragonsville was now faded by many tones from his adult splendour, though like a weathered cliff face, or ancient building, he had taken on the livery of age, and his rose and lavender were only dimmed to a gracious tenderness; yet one observed in the active newcomer a similar scheme of decoration, albeit in his somewhat stark magnificence he compared with the Lavender Dragon only as a new masterpiece resembles an old.

L.D. was still asleep when the discovery stirred his people; but Nicholas Warrender and Sir Claude Fortescue hastened to his couch with the extraordinary news, and though gouty and suffering some acute rheumatism in his left pinion, the dragon rose, looked out of the window, stared with increasing amazement and then left the Castle and strode out to accost the traveller.

It is to be noticed that the inherent suspicion planted in man against these creatures persisted, for, at sight of an unknown dragon, the people had fled to their homes and were now peeping from upper casements and dormer-windows to see what would come of this invasion. Those of faint heart already turned pale and feared the worst, "for," they whispered, "if this young and many-toothed dragon falls upon L.D., the issue is determined." But other parties took a different view. Some, the seneschal and the elders amongst them, believed that L.D. would prevail with fair speech and possibly make a swift convert of the stranger, even if his natural instincts inclined him to the immemorial rule of his kind; Sir Claude, ever a pessimist, thought not; others expected a grave disturbance, but believed that, given the forces of Dragonsville behind him, L.D. would deal faithfully with his young relation, if indeed a relation he proved to be. Of this company were Sir Jasper and George Pipkin. Indeed, the knight hastily donned his armour and rescued his helmet, which had lately been employed as a workbox for Petronell's embroideries, while the squire ran to bring in his steed and the piebald charger of his master. Both animals were far too fat, and George felt ashamed of their circular outlines as he led them under the Castle walls.

But there was no pitched battle, or any sort of disturbance. While the populace awaited with profound anxiety the coming event, L.D. approached his visitor, and though their gigantic preliminary embrace woke screams of terror from the fearful, it was clearly a matter of courtesy alone, for after the huge creatures became again disentangled, they walked up and down side by side in deep and not unfriendly converse. Clearly they argued a difficult problem, and presently they stopped and sat down together; but after two hours of close conference, and when, in anticipation of a good understanding, great feasts of hay, cider and sugared kidney beans had been prepared, the lesser dragon with a gesture of impatience and anger leapt to his feet, spat fire, spread his gorgeous wings and soared into the sky. A sensation of relief swept the beholders, but before they had time to surround their friend and learn particulars, he, too, opened glimmering vanes and, despite his rheumatism, flew heavily away after the other. Like twin clouds of rosy gold they swept eastward towards the risen sun and were soon lost to view.

Nor did L.D. return at nightfall, and many uneasy spirits slept not for thinking about this doubtful event. The seneschal and those who knew the master best judged that he had not prevailed with his kinsman and followed him in order to do so; but some dreaded a more sinister sequel to the incident and even suspected that the dragons were gone to fight beyond the reach of any interference. In the morning L.D. had not returned and, as day followed day, anxiety increased and despair awakened. A week passed and every face was dark, every heart heavy. The life of Dragonsville appeared to be suspended and the people, slighting good advice to go on with their work and trust Providence, wandered together in melancholy knots about the streets and public places, while every neck ached with straining backwards and every eye sickened at the sight of the empty sky. Father Lazarus did what he might and other leaders of opinion strove to say the word in season and keep hope alive; but all suffered severely and all were gratified when Sir Jasper and George Pipkin prepared to start eastward upon an expedition of search and succour.

Everybody applauded this resolve save Sir Claude Fortescue, who declared they should have started far sooner to be of service.

The morning for their departure had actually dawned and they were preparing to leave Dragonsville by its orient gate, when the Lavender Dragon came home alone. A sharp-eyed son of Sally Slater was the first to see him, and when the lad pointed to a tiny speck in the sky and yelled his glad discovery, others cuffed his ears for daring to waken hope; but he had seen truly; the speck darkened, then brightened and, in half an hour, the Lavender Dragon, flying very slowly, sank amidst his people, worn out and much dejected. They hastened round him, Doctor Doncaster leading the way. His patient was very lame and so feverish that the physician shook his head.

The dragon returned to his castle, ate a meal of clover hay, drank a hogshead of spring water and then addressed his friends.

"I have endured a bitter disappointment," he began. "In this younger being of my own race with whom I have fruitlessly spent the last week, I recognised a relation. He is, in fact, my nephew; and after seeing him upon my own territory, great hopes arose in me. I hastened to him, as you will remember, greeted him with large friendship and made him as welcome as I knew how. He had flown all night and was very hungry. He imagined that you dear people were my slaves—a sort of living larder from which I helped myself as appetite demanded. He declared himself to be starving and his first request was that I might send to him a dozen of the fat, prosperous children he had seen scampering from him on his arrival.

"I invited him to join me at breakfast and spoke of the glories of vegetarian diet. Whereupon he became abusive and said that he supposed his uncle to be a dragon, not a cow. I warned him that as he had come to Rome, he must do as Rome does, and fall in with my customs until he had opportunity to study them and perceive their dignity and worth; but he was ravenous and revealed all the overbearing habits of our race. Hunger, indeed, strips both men and dragons bare. He saw no charm whatsoever in my attitude of mind; he heard my principles with growing indignation. Then, calling me

'Impostor,' 'Renegade,' and so forth, he blew fire from his gullet, opened his wings and leapt from the ground in fury.

"But it is not my habit to yield at the first rebuff. He was a dragon of but one hundred years, and swiftly through my mind there flashed many an instance, gleaned from the annals of humanity, wherein we have seen the young sinner turn from evil and become a radiant convert. I thought upon Themistocles, who was cast out and disowned by his own father for his debaucheries and vile manner of life, yet became the most noble of all Greeks and a portent in Europe and Asia. I reflected on Valerius Flaccus, who from luxury and evil rose to be created Flamen and became as saintly a man as beforetime he was a rascal. I also remembered Polemo of Athens, saved from a life of scandal and a death of ignominy by the wisdom of Xenocrates, the philosopher, who charmed him to virtue and made of him a great and wise person. Did not Titus Vespasianus, from a cruel scoundrel become the darling and exemplar of mankind? And, to seek in the chronicles of Christianity, need we look farther than Saint Augustine, the Manichee, who, after an incontinent and lamentable youth, ascended by the ministry of Ambrose to salvation and saintship? These and other examples fortified hope, and so, taking thought for this son of a brother long departed, I spread wing and followed him.

"But it was all to no purpose whatsoever. He is an inveterate dragon of the prime, with bloody ideas and convictions that I could neither change nor shake. I persisted, however, until, losing his little store of patience, he turned upon me, cried that he held me as a craven abomination, doubtless in the pay of some accursed human monarch, and warned me that if I dogged his footsteps another day, he would forget what youth owed to age and turn and rend me. Indeed, he appeared doubtful whether it were not his duty to rid the world of 'a pestiferous and pusillanimous worm'—his own expression as nearly as I can translate it; and he declared that but for our relationship he should have done so at the first, and not suffered my bleating for five minutes.

"Worn out in body and mind, I left the callous reactionary, and were it not that he is my nephew, I should instantly direct you, Sir Jasper, to set out in quest of him and see whether your lance and spear cannot bring him in reach of reason. But I have decided to leave him with his reflections for the present. I may have done better than appeared. I live in faint hope that some of the good seed has taken root and will presently induce the fellow to return among us with an altered mind."

"I will go willingly," declared the knight. "It is to destroy just such a typical dragon as this that I set out upon my mission. Let us depart instantly, for my squire and I are equipped and were now about to seek you yourself."

But the weary monster would not sanction any immediate punitive expedition.

"Suffer a little time to pass," he said. "And now pull down the blinds and leave me. My foot must be fomented with a decoction of scalding poppies, and I will drink some physic; then, if the pain abates, I shall sleep for a couple of days and nights and probably awake restored."

As he foretold, the Lavender Dragon, once eased of his acute suffering, slumbered for eight-and-forty hours, and the reverberations from his nostrils rumbled like genial thunder in the ears of his thankful people during that period. At the end of this time he awoke refreshed, hungry and better of his ailment. Whereupon he took a bath in the morning sunshine, ate prodigiously and dismissed this unfortunate failure from his mind and conversation.

He was now in excellent humour and full of the approaching nuptials and the dwellings destined for the wedded pairs.

X

FROM JOY TO WOE

ON THE day before the double wedding, the Lavender Dragon was in a didactic mood, and said many interesting things which won the applause of some among his listeners but, as usual, made Sir Jasper, Sir Claude, Father Lazarus and other good men sad.

The monster spoke with his usual directness on the limitation of families.

"A great source of human unhappiness is over-crowding," he declared to them, "and here, as we know, it is agreed, with general accord, to expand in a ratio which bears directly upon the well-being and prosperity of all."

"You interfere with the liberty of the subject, Sir Dragon," ventured George Pipkin.

"That the liberty of the community shall not be interfered with, George," replied L.D. "The need to rear and fatten armies and navies for slaughter does not, you see, arise with us. We are a feeble, but not a fearful, folk, and we know that there are too many people in the world. Authority cannot cope with the increase and Nature does so—in a manner very painful to all of good will. Reason bewails the starved souls and bodies of many little ones, while superstition, patriotism and other faulty inspirations, still too much in evidence, clamour for more of these failures. It will presently, however, be driven into man's thick skull that quality is of greater force in affairs than quantity, and that war, famine and pestilence are cruel and abominable engines to keep the race in bounds. And when he makes this discovery, what will he do? He will first reach limitation of swords and spears, then, being a logical beast in his saner moments, attain to limitation of his own species. For when men compose their differences without shedding of blood, masses to murder and be murdered are an anachronism, and over-production becomes folly. It is argued that restriction may rob us of occasional great men. But can great men only be bred at cost of misery to thousands of small ones? If so, then let us struggle on without great men and rest content with the healthy and the sane. Our danger lies in the Orient world, whose fecundity is awful to contemplate and renders it a great obstacle to the security of the earth. East will not listen to the West on so delicate a subject, for Asia has family ideals and superstitions in this matter which must take centuries of time to dissipate."

"You want better bread than is made of wheat," said Sir Claude, and his voice was drearier than usual.

"Of course I do," replied the Lavender Dragon. "Most certainly I do; and you also, I should hope, and every man and woman who has a spirit worth calling one, and intelligence to measure things as they are. I deprecate discontent and covetousness as you will admit; but there is a discontent of the soul, Sir Claude, without which man is no better than the tadpole. Plenty of hearty, healthy children let us have by all means; and let us learn more from them and about them before we begin pouring in the varied and doubtful nonsense always on tap for their little, empty heads; let us wait in patience until they are ready to pronounce some opinion on the nostrums we hold to their infant lips."

"Do we not know far better than they, what is good for them, dear friend!" asked Father Lazarus.

"No, best of men, we do not," replied the dragon firmly. "I have studied the child for many hundreds of years, and I tell you this: the young are often far more reasonably minded than their parents. Nature leads them to take an honest view of life, and if that view is un-vitiated by grown-up lumber, it will not seldom develop and display a very rational estimate of conduct. But the work of our school-men in this virgin soil is often disastrous, and woe betide those who sow tares at that critical season when the rich material is best fitted to nourish and sustain them. To warp youthful intelligence and poison growing reason is a great fallacy and evil. There are precious, humanistic instincts of inquiry in well-nurtured and intelligent children, and that we should graft upon this spirit our questionable conclusions, rules of conduct, conventions, hatred of reality, chronic untruthfulness of outlook and imbecile pride, is utterly to spoil them in a very large proportion of cases. The potential power and value of many future men and women has thus been diminished; they are by so much rendered inferior, both as doers and thinkers. The stream of progress is dammed, the evolution of morals retarded. For, as I have often told you, the evolution of morals is a glorious fact; and that it should tend upwards is still more glorious; because upon this assurance hangs the destiny of mankind—all pessimists and doubters to the contrary notwithstanding. Let us, therefore, suffer the children to follow their bent, guarded and guided by pure reason; let us not catch them too young and foul the well-springs of their souls with a thousand uncertain and preposterous theories. Why, for example, does good Father Lazarus always agitate to get the children? Because he firmly believes that their future happiness and usefulness depend upon his doing so. He is much mistaken. Teach them to be clean, honest and faithful, just and merciful to the weak, humble, tolerant of others, scornful of self. Let them understand that certain instincts and temptations belong to their ancestry and original endowment; explain wherein good and evil consist according to our present worthiest values; but for the creeds and dogmas, the myths and magics, the mysteries and metaphysics, concerning which there is such an infinite diversity of opinion, let us spare them these until they reach years of discretion and are qualified to judge of their value to life and their correspondence with truth. This is not to weaken faith, but set it upon a basis of reason; for think not that faith and reason are opposed. Reason is founded upon our faith in all things reasonable."

Nicholas Warrender agreed with his master.

"Man is credulous enough through his aboriginal forefathers, without making him more so and teaching him to believe in goblins—good and bad—from his youth up," said the seneschal. "Thus you stain his dawning intellect, and soak it to such a colour that only one in a thousand ever gets the fabric of thought clean again. Remember that youth is the time of leisure, and when the young grow up, life and its immediate cares and occupations intervene, so that few have opportunity, let alone inclination, to go back and intelligently examine the opinions that have been implanted in them. They take these for granted henceforth, and bolt the doors of the mind upon inquiry. But what do you call them who decline to live behind bolted doors and seek for freedom instead? What name do you give to such as exercise liberty of thought and reject the learning thrust upon their infancy? 'Infidel' is the title reserved for such persons. Yet unto what are they unfaithful? Not to honour, justice, mercy, self-denial or charity. Only to the goblins. Thus the mass of men, who care not two pins for this subject, and whose sole concern is to prosper and preserve the approval of their neighbours, succeed in doing so, while such as honour their own gift of understanding and perceive these great and vital questions of religious faith and a world beyond the grave demand the very quintessence of their reverent examination, are cast out, persecuted, horribly destroyed for their pains, when and where the hierophants possess power to destroy them."

"And what is the melancholy result, my friends?" asked L.D. "In the Golden Age, the idea that religion should come between man and wisdom entered no head. The philosophers instructed and the sages questioned and argued without let and hindrance; for then it was understood that progress depended upon the spirit of inquiry. But now, alas! official and state-supported superstitions block this spirit at every turn; prosperous error bars the way to afflicted truth, and he who approaches these profound subjects through any other road than that pointed out for him by his rulers will soon find himself a trespasser on forbidden ground."

"All religions are as scaffolding, and our children's children will yet see the scaffolding pulled down," declared Nicholas Warrender. "These opinions are yet in the tide of their career, but must presently remain with us only as the useless hair upon our bodies and the tell-tale fragments of our anatomy which point to purposes now outworn."

"Consider," added the dragon, "how many shapes man has given to his divinities. It was long before he exalted God to his own image. He ransacked the categories of Nature before he conceived those august forms of the later and human pantheons beyond which he cannot go. The Egyptians worshipped Apis, the ox; at Arsinoe, the crocodile was deity; in the city of Hercules, the ichneumon. Others adored a cat, an ibis, a falcon. The people of Hispanola kneel to invisible fairies and pray to them under the name of Zemini. In the Isle of Java the thing first met of a morning is the god for the day, no matter whether a reptile, beast or fowl. Those of Manta have made an emerald the Everlasting, and offer prayer and pilgrimage to it, bringing the inevitable gifts which the priesthood of that precious stone know how to charm from them. The Romans created a goddess of a city, and the people of Negapatam built their Pagod, a massy monster drawn upon a chariot of many wheels and over-laid with gold. The warlike Alani worship a naked sword, which is the only god they know who can answer their petitions; and in Ceylon, upon the peak of Adam, is kept the tooth of an ape—held by the Cingalese to be the holiest thing and the most potent in all Asia. With a more noble faith do the Assyrians confront us, for they worshipped the Sun and the Earth, from which they received life. The dove was sacred among them; it is a symbol still held in holiest esteem among the Christians, as you know. At Ekron the Lord of Flies enjoyed first place, and Baal-zebub, the Larder-god, doubtless received many prayers to keep his myriads under control. Those of Peru adored the corpses of their Emperors, and ancestor worship persists among certain Oriental people unto this day.

"A thousand other manifestations of divinity are in the knowledge of the learned before we come to the solitary god of the Jew—a Being nobly exalted and purified, but, even as the Allah of Mahomet, One still all too human in his essence and behaviour. These deities occupied my profound attention and I made this discovery concerning the different interpretations put upon them, that not Absolutism or Idealism, not Immanentism or Pragmatism, or any other 'ism,' or scism whatsoever, will lead mankind's few and uncertain footsteps through his short life to happiness, or security. To suppose, as these people do, that their gods possess the potency, impatience and self-ishness of Oriental panjandrums is vain; and whether such Eternal

Beings are transcendent or immanent, universal or particular, matters nothing at all. What does matter is that they are not gentlemen; and to how parlous a state must that divinity be reduced who can learn manners, discipline and conduct from the like of us! The gods who behave worse than their creatures and make it needful that their chosen ministers should forever apologise and explain their unsocial conduct, are not gods; for right must be right and wrong must be wrong, whether committed by a deity or a dragon; and if it be admitted that these Supreme Beings know how to choose, direct and control with utmost wisdom and purest virtue, what shall be thought while they themselves, in their almighty power, daily perpetrate or sanction abominations for which the world would execrate any child of man?

"Then you, my own dear Christians, have discovered a triune God—Three in One and One in Three. And who shall presume to question your convictions if you abide in them peacefully, without hating and murdering other people who cannot see eye to eye with you? Truth asks for nothing but open and honourable warfare against Falsehood. Given a fair field, she cannot be defeated. The story will reach its conclusion, however, because, when there is a means of return to independence, freedom with security, and consequent renewed progress, mankind must be swift to take that way. We shall presently see philosophers, each with his personal God. They will write books about their deities and every one will seek to show how his own concept of the Eternal transcends all others. Some of these home-made divinities may not be all powerful; some will even depend upon their creatures to strengthen their knees and help their difficult task. They are much to the good—these personal gods conceived by clever and earnest people, even though no two of them will ever have more than a family resemblance. Time does not stand still, and evolution continues to do her perfect work."

But the Christians had all stolen away, led by Sir Claude and Father Lazarus. The dragon found only his seneschal still left to listen; and he was not listening: the old man had gone to sleep.

A glorious autumn day dawned for the weddings, and Dragons-ville made holiday. Only those whose duty it was to milk the cows and feed the cattle put a hand to work, and though it was impossible for L.D. to go to church, the building not being constructed to admit him, he sat just outside with his huge head on the earth, where he might listen to the marriage service and the admirable address delivered to the wedded couples by Father Lazarus. In this exordium the good priest took occasion to traverse sharply and caustically many of the Lavender Dragon's own most cherished sentiments; but the monster felt no unkindly emotion before such an attack. He loved Father Lazarus and never quarrelled with the least person who declined to share his own ideas. Any sort of persecution caused him violent uneasiness, for he held that nothing excused loss of temper and cruelty, fanaticism and intolerance.

L.D. fell into error at the banquet which followed the nuptials and, despite his doctor's entreaties, drank far too much cider and ate too many sugared kidney beans.

After all was consumed, the dragon went into his treasure house and produced wedding gifts and also presents for everybody, to the least infant on his mother's lap.

"I cannot give the little ones anything they value," exclaimed L.D. to Sir Jasper, "for the idea of property vanishes in a generation or two when once human nature begins to share the ethical purity of the ant. It is better to want than to have; it is better still not to want. They do not want. But you see everybody takes my gifts for my sake; and you must do the same. These jewels are of priceless value, according to the world's opinion, but of none whatever in Dragonsville. Even for beauty, a necklace of bluebells beats them hollow."

The happy couples departed for their honeymoons in a distant part of the kingdom half a day's ride from town. There, in a notable spot known as the Valley of Ferns, stood two bungalows sacred to the newly wed, and in this sequestered and attractive region the Lady Pomeroy and Mrs. George Pipkin wandered very happily with their husbands.

Then they returned to hear sad news, which at L.D.'s orders had been kept from their ears until they did so.

The Lavender Dragon had fallen dangerously ill with an attack of gout, which involved not only his four gigantic paws, but threatened his vitals also.

A gloom as of eclipse sat upon the faces of the people. All merry-making had ceased; even the children only played the quietest games and could put little heart into their pleasure.

XI

THE PASSING

BY SLOW and gradual stages the Lavender Dragon approached his end. Sometimes he rallied, and the gallons of colchicum which he consumed, while rendering him very languid, sufficed to lessen his misery. Now and then he was lifted onto a gigantic trolley and dragged for half a mile through the gardens, that he might take the air and see the people; but his activities were over, and though his mind continued clear and his spirit cheerful, his body lost all strength and he knew that he would never take wing again. To the prospect of a final flight under the sunshine he clove for a long while; then he abandoned the hope with rational resignation.

"It is good," he said, "that we do not know when we perform a well-loved action for the last time. Ignorance in such a matter is mercy, for, looking back after many days, we can bear the knowledge that must have wakened active grief at the moment. . . ."

He was in a pensive mood on an occasion when Sir Jasper and Petronell sat beside him and cheered him with their conversation.

"Fate," he said, "has an art to take what we most value and deny the summit of our ambition, while granting gifts small by comparison in our eyes, though infinitely precious to others, who lack them. He who desires fame is offered wealth, or love. The hungry for love may win to high place by their art, or craft, yet would gladly barter it for the female they dream about. The genius goes childless, though like enough he would thankfully sacrifice his master endowment for little children on his knee; while the man with a full quiver yearns for that peace and lack of responsibility which he supposes would enable him to do great deeds. It is in fact a sad but blessed human quality to covet what lies beyond our reach. The content are ever negligible, for only frozen sympathies and peddling minds can be so."

He spoke of the Latin god, Pan, with great affection, and declared himself to be in union and understanding with that divinity.

"But in Pan lurks a peril against which you must guard," warned the dragon. "There is a panic terror, a fear and dread of him, that may awake at any moment to ruin life; and there is a panic trust, equally destructive—that blind, cowardly repose in his shadow which tends to rob us of self-command and self-expression. Both these extremes stultify existence, and other gods than Pan are also responsible for them."

Sometimes the fading monster was in a cheerful humour and delighted to tell stories. Indeed he never tired of doing so until the end, and children were admitted to him, fifty at a time, to listen while he related the fables and historic tales they loved.

On one such occasion the little sons of Sally Pipkin replied, when he asked what he should tell the young people assembled, and begged for the narrative of the Jeweller.

"I too, like that story," answered the dragon, "and am well pleased to rehearse it once again. A certain jeweller in the time of Galienus displayed a soup-tureen of exquisite workmanship, which he declared was wrought of a single ruby; and the Empress, doting on the treasure, prevailed with the Emperor Galienus to purchase it for her. To please his lass was the Caesar's first delight at all times; so he paid a mighty price for the soup-tureen, and the jeweller, who had long desired a snug villa on the Sabine Hills, now retired from business and prepared to spend the remainder of his life among his vines and olives in luxury and ease.

"But there came a man from the East, of great wisdom in all jewels and precious things, and having heard concerning this wonder he went to court and prayed that it might be permitted him to gladden his eyes with the ruby soup-tureen—a jewel beyond even his experience. Aware of the Oriental's fame, he was made welcome by Galienus and permitted to see the magnificent collections of the royal palace; and then, after he had beheld and admired a thousand works of art and nature, the crowning glory was placed in his hands and he examined the soup-tureen carved of a single ruby.

"But no word of praise rewarded this masterpiece. Instead, the wise man frowned, sighed heavily, and making obeisance to the Empress, addressed her with Eastern politeness and wrapped his harsh news in flowery words.

"He declared that, from the first, he had suspected fraud, because a ruby of size to make a soup-tureen was clean contrary to Nature. And now his fears had been too bitterly confirmed, for the soup-tureen was only glass. It possessed small intrinsic value and no interest whatever, excepting of a tragical and painful character.

"Thereupon the Empress ran to the Emperor with many tears, and Galienus, a just prince, despatched swift soldiers to the jeweller's villa, arrested the rascal as he was about to eat his dinner, and hastened him to a dungeon.

"At a later hour he stood before the outraged Emperor and heard his doom. 'What,' enquired Galienus, 'shall be done to him who robs his monarch and fools the Queen? The least, I think, would be that he should make a Roman holiday. In a word, guilty man, you will only see the light of day again upon the sands of the stadium at our next festivity.'

"With this dreadful promise the guilty jeweller was hustled from his sovereign's presence, nothing left to hope for but a terrible and uncertain death; and he had no support in his trial and no consciousness of right behind him to assist his spirit through the evil hours that still remained. For very well indeed he knew that the soup-tureen was glass, since he had himself designed and executed it in secret.

"Not long was the jeweller called to wait execution of sentence, for on the third day after arrest he found himself blindfolded, led away and presently permitted to see again. He now stood on the sand of the amphitheatre amid an immense concourse of his fellow country-men, while above him, in the royal box, sat the deluded Empress and her spouse, together with the notables of Rome about them.

"Only one other creature shared that bitter expanse of sand with the jeweller. It was a huge, African lion with black mane and tawny pelt; and the spectators, who had thronged the place to see this gaunt monster already waiting for his prey, felt no little astonishment that a lion, kept without food for a week, should hesitate before the plump and succulent spectacle of the erring jeweller now within his reach.

"Yet, for a time the ferocious beast moved not, but sat with its green, unblinking eyes upon the sinner. It opened its mouth, to reveal a formidable circle of white fangs, and it slowly swept the dust with its tufted tail. But, as a sybarite, who delays his delicious morsel for the pleasure of anticipation, the lion still delayed. The jeweller also delayed and made no effort to shorten the distance between him-self and the instrument of punishment, until a voice—the Emper-or's own—was lifted in command. He ordered the victim to save the lion further trouble and the company longer delay. Whereupon the doomed man, himself weary of such horrid suspense, crept—a stout, solitary figure in a blue toga—to the denizen of the desert.

"The crouching lion lashed his tail, and the man came nearer and nearer, until he stood within half a yard of his destroyer's gaping jaws. Doubtless he then felt that the monster might be invited to do the rest. But thereupon an astounding thing happened, for Galienus himself, to the horror of his wife and the company, leapt alone and unarmed into the arena and joined the shaking criminal and the lion appointed to devour him. Then, in a loud and cheerful voice which reached all corners of that mighty concourse, the Emperor spoke.

"'May it please you, my august wife, my ministers and my dear people, to learn what this mystery means. I have, as you well know, been ever of opinion that the punishment should fit the crime; and upon hearing this fat rascal was a cheat, it struck me that to cheat him again would be a very just and proper reward for his villainy. He thought that he was going to die and make a meal for a fine and hungry lion. Well, he's sold, for this lion is but a thing of putty, paint and straw, with a cunning contrivance inside him to make him open his jaws and wag his tail.'

"Galienus kicked the lion as he spoke and the effigy toppled over upon its side; he then kicked the jeweller and told him to be off and mend his abominable ways. Whereupon the thankful fellow fell on his knees, kissed the purple shoon of his monarch and scuttled sweating from the arena amid roars of laughter.

"But whether the Empress laughed we know not, for it may have been a joke for which she lacked the necessary humour. Galienus, however, won the applause of a vast majority on that occasion, since empires can easiest bear the yoke of tyrants who enjoy a sense of fun."

The children lifted their voices in familiar delight, for this was a story that never wearied them, and they were not saddened by the knowledge that L.D. would never tell it again.

On another occasion the seneschal, Sir Claude, Doctor Doncaster and other of the elders invited the Lavender Dragon to indicate his wishes for the future, concerning which there existed much difference of opinion among them.

"First," said Warrender, "we most desire to render your own great name immortal."

The Lavender Dragon smiled and considered the subject with closed eyes; then, according to his wont, he traced parallel instances from history when a like problem had arisen.

He drank a huge jorum of colchicum and spoke to them.

"You remind me of ingenious men who have desired that their fame should shine after they had gone beyond reach of it. There was that Seventh wonder of the world which Sostratus built for

Ptolemy Philadelphus. 'The Tower of Pharos' it was called, and in secret the architect wrote upon it: 'Sostratus to the gods, and for the safety of sailors'; but these words, carved in enduring stone, he hid behind a covering of plaster inscribed with the name and title and glory of Ptolemy. And this he did, well knowing that the waves of the sea would presently wash the monarch's claim away and reveal his own name engraved on marble for subsequent generations. Yet where is that Pharos now? Again, when Alexander the Great threw down the walls of Thebes, Phryne offered to rebuild them at her own charges, provided that she might record thereon how Alexander had destroyed and Phryne had restored. Remember, too, Trajan, who set his name on every stone he erected, until the wits gave him a new name, and called him 'Pellitory of the Wall.'

"No, my dear Nicholas, and you, my good friends," he continued. "I have not the least desire for posthumous honour, or to be remembered save by the kind hearts that have beaten with my own and aided my endeavour. As to the future, they often have ill-fortune who seek to tie up the time to come with dead hands. For the future will not be dictated to, and no man can prophesy how human values may change, or say when one kingdom shall desire a monarch, another a republic and a third anarchy. True it is that we groan and labour under dead laws and the decayed enactments of vanished generations and pestilential precedents; but that is only because for the most part we richly reward the knaves who enforce them, and the nation as a whole is too ignorant, or lazy, to cast off its burden.

"You remind me of an Emperor of Constantinople, Anastasius by name, who, being short of friends and well knowing that his time was at hand, paused to reflect on his successor. Near issue he had none, and the choice lay between three nephews—brothers, concerning whom he knew little good, or ill. In his esteem they were equal; and since reason could not decide between them, he trusted to chance, for he caused three beds to be set in a sleeping chamber and hid the empire's crown in the tester of one. Then, sending for the boys, he entertained them and, when night was come, bade them go sleep and choose which bed they would. With morn the Emperor himself entered the apartment of the brothers, to learn which had reposed beneath the crown. And what did he discover? The eldest boy slumbered in a bed innocent of the diadem; and to the second, whose sleep also was not frowned upon by the awful symbol, had crept his smallest brother—for company. The regal couch lay untenanted."

"A good tale," said the seneschal, "but no answer, L.D."

"When I chanced upon my own nephew, not so long ago," confessed the dragon, "I own a passing inspiration flashed to my brain and led me to wonder if, by good hap, he might be disposed to carry on our labours and consent to take my place and uphold my tradition. But, as you know, any hope in that direction swiftly vanished. Nor will I even emulate Julian, the Emperor, and leave the helm to him your living judgments may approve. It pleases me better to think that Dragonsville shall be thrown open to the world, and that our modest enterprise may be seen and considered for what it is worth by all men of good will. Let the young go forth and carry with them our principles, and let the middle-aged and old, if they so will, remain here and illustrate them. Let it be shown how that happiness is only real which has been procured by a man for his fellow man; let a community be discovered that is actuated by this rule of conduct. Invite the people to survey Dragonsville, since herein lies our proof; and ask the mighty and the wise and those inspired with love for their kind to determine whether or no our theories admit of application on a more generous scale. Perhaps not; it may be that only such a primitive folk as ourselves, satisfied with little and no longer stung by lust of possession, could pursue this ingenuous manner of life; but much might be done, and I die firmly persuaded that if we could but strike at the root of man's selfishness, his superstition and his egregious desire to prosper at the expense of everybody else, then substantial progress would be merely a question of time. I have lived to see the two bitterest enemies of man, and their names are Greed and Creed; while the handmaid of their happiness, the Cinderella that toils for them with little thanks, and still waits patiently to become their queen, is Reason. And, sooner or later, she will assuredly reign over a united earth, since without reason unity is impossible."

Within a few weeks of this speech, and after another winter's frost was melted out of the ground, the dragon directed that his grave should be begun.

"It will take a long time," he said, "and I should like to see it finished."

Therefore, with many tears (for this business impressed upon them what was soon to happen), the people began to dig a mighty pit, one hundred yards long, twenty-five yards broad and twenty yards deep. It yawned beside the grove of budding hawthorns which covered the tumulus of his wife; and L.D. lived to see the scented glory of the may before he passed.

There was an incident at the early digging and, for the first and only time, Dicky Gollop, the jester, made the Lavender Dragon laugh. For while the monster inspected his grave, as yet but five feet deep, Dicky failed to see where he was stepping and fell in backwards. Thus at last he reached to his ambition, though in a left-handed sort of manner, and genuinely entertained his master.

After the completion of this work the Lavender Dragon failed rapidly, and there came a day in June when with the dawn he died. About him were assembled the seneschal and other old men and women, Father Lazarus, Sir Jasper and Petronell, Sir Claude and Doctor Doncaster, who ministered to the expiring monster. The Lavender Dragon's last words were not forgotten by those who heard them.

"Fetch the trolley, while I have strength to crawl upon it," he said. "It will save you much trouble afterwards."

They obeyed, and with an expiring effort, L.D. stretched his bulk upon the vehicle and lost consciousness. His heart heaved behind the mighty ribs a little longer; then the beat grew slow and stopped; the blinds of his lids rolled down slowly over the fading opals of his eyes, and he was quite dead.

XII

BUTTERFLIES

UPON THE night after the funeral, as though to indicate that the old order had changed for ever, the walls of Dragonsville fell to the earth and the empire of the Lavender Dragon ceased to exist as a separate kingdom, defended and preserved behind its own ramparts. An immense restlessness already infected the people, and when it was known that the walls had crumbled, many feared and many rejoiced. The young would lead away their kinsfolk into the outer world, and not a few consented to accompany them; but others remained and hoped that they might be permitted to do so. Of these were Nicholas Warrender, who took now the lead at the wish of all, with George Pipkin for his right-hand man. Sir Claude of the Strong Shield also determined to spend the balance of his time in tending the dragon's grave.

As for Sir Jasper of Pomeroy and his fair wife, they set forth on a cloudless morning in hope to find welcome and waken far-spreading happiness at home in the West-country; while many from Pongley-in-the-Marsh and elsewhere also returned to their places, somewhat over-sanguine that the message of goodwill and good tidings they brought might reconcile their heirs to their return.

Father Lazarus remained at Dragonsville, and it was in connection with this honourable and faithful man that the first hard words were spoken within that township after the decease of the founder.

Sir Jasper was just about to depart upon his long journey southward when this unfortunate thing happened. He rode his piebald charger, and Lady Petronell sat beside him on her riding-horse, a powerful and mettlesome beast. One accompanied them, having his own steed and a second, whereon their trifling luggage was bestowed. He was a lad born and bred at Dragonsville, who had entered the knight's service. The priest, with Nicholas Warrender,

Sir Claude, George Pipkin and many others, collected to bid the voyagers god-speed, and as he drank the stirrup cup, Sir Jasper spoke of their departed friend.

"May his humane and gentle spirit enter into us, and help us to advance the happiness of a weary world," said he.

"It has done so," declared his wife. "None who enjoyed knowledge of our dear dragon can ever be quite the same afterwards."

"Be sure that we shall yet welcome him in a place of perfect happiness when it is our turn," asserted Sir Claude with an unusual ray of hope; but Father Lazarus sighed and refused to echo any such sentiment.

"A vain aspiration," he answered. "We must be brave in this matter and not palter with conscience. None can feel greater grief than myself to recognise the truth; but the truth is ever unassailable. In a word, L.D. has gone where the bad dragons go, since there is no appointed place for good dragons, and it were vain to deceive ourselves and pretend otherwise. To this fate is he fallen, not because he himself was bad—far from it—I never met such a saintly character on two feet, let alone four; but because, having brain and wit to choose the right path, he preferred to remain upon the wrong one; and virtue is of nothing worth that springs from foundations that will not bear the test of Faith."

The seneschal snorted, and Sir Jasper spoke.

"Haply he will be pitied and pardoned in credit of his good works," ventured the knight.

"Alas! We have the highest authority for refusing to believe any such thing," replied Father Lazarus sadly. "He would be the first to own it himself."

"Out on you!" cried Nicholas Warrender, his eye flashing and his white beard a-bristle. "What manner of man are you to deny salvation to your benefactor and first friend? Did not the Almighty make you both, and make him worth a thousand of you?"

They wrangled so that they forgot to bid the parting pair "farewell," and Sir Jasper, who lacked not sympathy for either side, rode forward with his wife and left them to it. But neither convinced the other, since they had entered upon that age-long argument, wherein only a time yet to come shall declare the victory.

* * * * *

For six generations after his disappearance the dragon's grave continued to be a scene of pilgrimage; and then his rede was forgotten and the things he had attempted to do no longer remembered. He sank into a myth, and his castle and his city crumbled away under the sleights of time. The owl hooted in his dining hall; the bat hung aloft in his sleeping chamber; and presently the ivy, with steadfast might, dragged all down until not one stone remained upon another. Then did the watchful Woods of Blore, finding no hindrance, creep forward with sapling legions that swiftly bulked to trees and so engulfed and swallowed that happy valley, until all evidence of man and his labour alike disappeared.

Yet even to this day, at the season of high summer, the wanderer with faith may chance upon a knoll still open to the sky, and find the great mound bright in a robe of scented lavender, agleam with vanessa butterflies—black and scarlet, crimson and purple. The living jewels dance in sunshine and fragrance, and round about sing birds and patter the furry creatures of the wild.

Beneath lie the bones of a vast saurian—that excellent mystery known to the Dark Ages as the Lavender Dragon; and since all history is but an echo and a reverberation, it may happen that his theory shall yet revive to challenge the mind of man, and his practice be again attempted.

We have made a measure of progress since the days of Dragonsville, and the fact that we are so widely, keenly alive to the need for yet swifter advance is the most hopeful thing about us. There speaks the evolution of our moral nature, wakening from long dalliance; there moves the spirit of good will, struck into a cruel coma by the torment of recent years. Mighty powers are they, to help humanity correct its values, purify its ambitions and seek those ideals of generosity, abnegation and selfless purpose, without which no pathway of advancement through darkness into day can be discovered. Dawn is upon the mountain tops and, as the sun arises, light will descend into the homes and heart of mankind—because it can do no other.